"Were your sneakers in the locker room last night?" Coach Allen asked Joe.

"Yes," Joe said, "but my feet are fine."

"That's weird," said Hank. "Why would everyone else have itching powder in his sneakers, but not you?"

Joe had been wondering the same thing, but he hadn't come up with an answer that made sense.

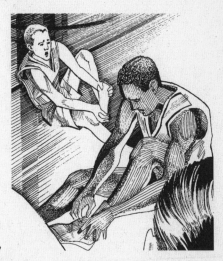

"I think I know," Damont said. He turned to Joe with a look that made Joe feel suddenly ill at ease. "Maybe it's because Joe did it."

"What!" Joe cried.

"You heard me," said Damont in an accusing tone. "I think you put that itching powder in everyone's sneakers."

Other books in the
wishbone™ Mysteries series:

WISHBONE Mysteries

THE MALTESE DOG

by Anne Capeci

WISHBONE™ created by Rick Duffield

Big Red Chair Books™, *A Division of **Lyrick Publishing**™*

This book is a work of fiction. The characters, incidents, and dialogues are products of the author's imagination and are not to be construed as real. Any resemblance to actual events or persons, living or dead, is entirely coincidental.

 Big Red Chair Books™, *A Division of **Lyrick Publishing**™*
300 E. Bethany Drive, Allen, Texas 75002

©1998 Big Feats! Entertainment

Edited by Pam Pollack

Copy edited by Jonathon Brodman

Cover concept and design by Lyle Miller

Interior illustrations by Genevieve Meek

Wishbone photograph by Carol Kaelson

Library of Congress Catalog Card Number: 97-74834

ISBN: 1-57064-486-1

First printing: March 1998

10 9 8 7 6 5 4 3 2 1

For Jonathan, Danny, and Marissa

FROM THE BIG RED CHAIR . . .

Oh . . . hi! Wishbone here. You caught me right in the middle of some of my favorite things—books. Let me welcome you to the WISHBONE MYSTERIES. In each story, I help my human friends solve a puzzling mystery. In *THE MALTESE DOG*, someone is playing practical jokes on the basketball team—and the guys suspect my pal Joe! Joe and I must clear his name fast, before the pranks split the team apart.

The story takes place late in the fall, during the same time period as the events you'll see in the second season of my WISHBONE television show. In this story, Joe is fourteen, and he and his friends are in the eighth grade. Like me, they are always ready for adventure . . . and a good mystery.

You're in for a real treat, so pull up a chair and a snack and sink your teeth into *THE MALTESE DOG*.

Chapter One

Wishbone wagged his tail and trotted along the sidelines in front of rows of metal bleachers in the Sequoyah Middle School gym. The smell of sweat and the feeling of excitement were in the air. Boys charged up and down the basketball court, dribbling and passing the ball. The game was so exciting that the white-with-brown-and-black-spots Jack Russell terrier could hardly keep himself from running out into the thick of the action to play with them. Could there possibly be a better way to spend a Tuesday evening? Wishbone didn't think so.

"*Great* defense, Joe!" Wishbone's alert brown eyes followed a boy whose uniform had the number 20 on it. That was fourteen-year-old Joe Talbot, Wishbone's very best buddy—and a fantastic basketball player. Joe's face was red from all the action, and his brown hair plastered to his forehead. He kept his arms open wide, waving them in every direction to prevent the forward from the other team from passing the ball or shooting a basket.

"Let's hear it for the Sequoyah Bulldogs!" cried a boy in the stands. "Hip, hip . . ."

Wishbone barked his "Hooray!" along with the rest of the crowd. Maybe bulldogs weren't quite as handsome as terriers, but Wishbone wasn't going to let that stop him from cheering Joe's team on to victory. After all, he himself had become the official team mascot after the original mascot, a bulldog named Otis, had moved away from Oakdale. Wishbone even wore an official sweater with the Bulldogs's team colors, blue with a big gold "S" on it.

"Pretty exciting, eh, guys?" Wishbone gave a big doggie smile to Joe's mom, Ellen Talbot. She was sitting in the front row with Samantha Kepler, one of Joe and Wishbone's two best friends.

"The Bulldogs are down by one point," Sam said. She was so tense that she bit her lip. Wishbone liked Sam very much. She loved to have fun and adventure as much as he did. And she always had a treat or a friendly pat for him. She was wearing jeans, a blue turtleneck sweater, and a baseball cap from Pepper Pete's, the pizza parlor her father owned. Sam's blond hair was pulled back in a ponytail, but Wishbone couldn't see much of her face. It was mostly hidden by the camera Sam held, snapping pictures of the game.

"How about a shot of the team mascot, Sam?" Wishbone stood up on his hind legs and rested his chin and paws on Sam's leg, and she scratched him behind the ears. "Ah, that feels good. A little to the left . . . Perfect!"

"Just fifteen seconds left on the clock," said the announcer over the loudspeaker system.

Wishbone smiled when he saw David Barnes talking into the microphone at the announcer's table, beneath the scoreboard. "Hi, David! Keep up the good work."

David was Wishbone and Joe's other best friend. He announced all the Bulldogs's games. In Wishbone's opinion, David was the perfect person for the job. He was fair, responsible, and very nice. And he, too, often had a special treat for the official team mascot.

"Fifteen seconds?" Joe's mom frowned as she looked out at the court. "If the Bulldogs don't get the ball soon, we're going to lose!"

"Lose?" Wishbone cocked his head to one side, glancing up at Ellen. "Don't even think about it!"

The forward from the other team started to pass to one of his teammates. As soon as the ball left the player's fingertips, Joe made his move. His hands shot out, and he grabbed the basketball in midair.

"He did it!" Sam cried. She jumped to her feet, snapping more photos. "Oakdale's got the ball!"

Talk about speedy! thought Wishbone. *And there isn't even any kibble involved! 'Atta boy, Joe!*

Joe's sneakers let out a loud squeak as he spun around and headed toward the other team's basket.

The crowd roared, counting down the final seconds of the game. "Ten! Nine! Eight . . ."

"Come on!" Sam murmured under her breath. "You can do it. . . ."

Wishbone's tail wagged. "Go! Go! Go! Go!"

A wall of players stampeded toward Joe. They looked just as determined as Wishbone usually was to get leftover scraps after dinner.

Wishbone could hardly bring himself to watch. "Hey! Didn't anyone ever teach you guys that it isn't polite to crowd?"

Just when it seemed the other team would bury Joe, he twisted around them. The ball flew from Joe's hands in a perfect bounce-pass to one of his teammates, Damont Jones. Wishbone knew from experience that Damont wasn't always the nicest person. But he was a great basketball player.

As Damont caught the ball, the crowd's roar became deafening. Damont dribbled the ball once, then sent it flying through the air toward the basket.

"Three! Two . . ."

The basketball *whooshed* through the hoop. A split-second later the buzzer sounded. The game was over.

"We won!" cried Sam. She and Ellen jumped up and down, hugging each other.

"Yippee!" Wishbone was so proud he leaped up in the air and did his best flip. "You realize I taught Joe everything he knows," he said to Sam and Ellen. "I knew all that training with my balls and squeaky toys in the backyard would pay off!" Rising up on his hind legs, Wishbone barked at Ellen and Sam. "How about a high paw, guys?"

Sam and Ellen slapped their palms together over Wishbone's head.

Wishbone sighed. "No one ever listens to the dog."

Then Wishbone saw the basketball rolling across the gym floor, and he perked up again.

"Now that the game is over, can *I* play with that?"

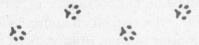

An hour later, Wishbone trotted proudly down the sidewalk in downtown Oakdale. There was a chill in the November air, but Wishbone's sleek fur kept him warm. Walking behind him were Joe, Sam, David, and Ellen. All of them wore jackets.

"Let's hear it for the Bulldogs's conquering hero, Joe Talbot!" Wishbone gave his best friend a big doggie grin. "He's fast, he's brave, he's—"

"Wow! Am I starved!" said Joe.

"He's starved! Now that you mention it, I'm about ready for dinner myself." Wishbone tilted up his nose and sniffed. "Isn't that pepperoni? That must mean we're at . . . Yes! Pepper Pete's. My favorite place to eat out!"

11

"Get ready for all the pizza you can eat," said Ellen as she pulled open the door to the pizza parlor. "After the way you played today, Joe, you deserve it. I'm really proud of you."

"You were awesome," Sam chimed in. "We just had our third straight win, thanks to that steal you made."

Wishbone sensed a new presence with his always sensitive nose. He looked back to see Damont Jones coming up behind them, wearing his Bulldogs jacket. Damont's younger cousin, ten-year-old Jimmy Kidd, was walking with him. When Damont saw Joe, a smirk spread across his face. "You mean, thanks to the great shot *I* made," he said.

"Yeah," Jimmy piped up. "Damont is the best."

Wishbone didn't know Jimmy all that well, but he had seen him at the basketball courts in Jackson Park whenever Damont played. Jimmy spent a lot of time at the school gym, too, when there was basketball practice. In fact, Jimmy seemed to worship his cousin. He followed Damont *everywhere*. Of course, Wishbone knew Jimmy's chihuahua, Dinky, a lot better. They had gone digging together in the same earthy spots more than a few times.

"If Joe hadn't stolen the ball, you wouldn't have had a chance to make that shot, Damont," David pointed out.

Damont shrugged. "Whatever." He flicked a thumb at the brand-new, ultra-high-tech, blue-and-white sneakers that hung from Joe's shoulder by their laces. "Cool sneakers. But I don't think they'll make you a better player than I am."

"Hey! You can't talk to Joe like that." Wishbone looked up sharply at Damont, but Damont stepped past him and disappeared inside Pepper Pete's. Jimmy was right behind him.

"Joe, it was a team effort that won the game," said Ellen.

"He did make the winning basket," Joe said.

"Hmm . . . But he didn't win that game by himself," Sam said. "I don't know why he won't admit you were just as responsible for today's win as he was."

"Speaking of which . . . How about a little credit for Joe's personal trainer?" Tail wagging, Wishbone headed toward the open door. "My very own pizza would be a great way to say thanks. I was thinking of a double pepperoni with—"

That was when Wishbone spotted her—a white Yorkshire terrier coming out of the alley next to Pepper Pete's. Wishbone stopped short, his paws frozen to the sidewalk.

Look at that silky fur . . . that cute nose . . . those outstanding eyes! She's the most beautiful creature on four legs!

Wishbone trotted over to the terrier. "Hi, there! Are you new in town? I don't think I've ever seen you before."

Yorkie sat down and gazed at Wishbone. Her tail wagged in anticipation. Her brown eyes were filled with such intrigue . . . adventure! One look at them, and Wishbone wanted to follow her through every flower bed in Oakdale.

"Wishbone!" Joe called. "Come on, boy. If you want pizza, you'd better come now."

Wishbone hesitated. Pizza . . . or Yorkie?

13

Yorkie barked and then scampered back down the alleyway. She stopped, turned to face Wishbone, and barked again. As he looked into her doggie eyes once more, Wishbone made up his mind.

"You want to play, Yorkie? Count me in! Catch you later, Joe! I'll meet you back here in a little while." Wishbone ran after Yorkie, his tongue wagging at full speed. "So, what kinds of games do you like? Chasing your tail? Digging up bones . . . ?"

Chapter Two

Joe stopped in front of his locker after his last class on Wednesday. He spun the combination, pulled open the door, and dumped his books inside. He was just grabbing his sports bag when someone spoke up behind him.

"Great game yesterday, Joe."

Looking over his shoulder, Joe recognized a girl from his English class. "Thanks," he told her.

Joe felt as if he hadn't stopped smiling since last night's big win. He'd been working hard to improve his game. Now that he was starting to get noticed, he had to admit it felt good. Maybe he would never be as flashy as Damont, but he liked knowing he was an important part of the team.

"Hey, Joe," said Samantha, coming up to him. "I think I got some great photos of the game. I'm going to develop the film this afternoon." She started to hold up a roll, then stopped when she saw a book Joe was taking out of his locker. "You're reading *The Maltese Falcon*? That's by Dashiell Hammett, isn't it?"

"Yes." Joe handed her the dog-eared copy. "It was in the box of mysteries that belonged to my dad."

Joe liked to dig through the books he'd found in a box in their attic. They had belonged to his dad, who had died when Joe was younger. There were some by Agatha Christie, Edgar Allan Poe, Arthur Conan Doyle, Dashiell Hammett—all the classic mystery authors. Joe had read only a few so far. But he was determined to get through all of them eventually. Somehow, reading the books made Joe feel closer to his dad.

"Cool," said Sam, flipping through the yellowed pages. "My father read this. It's about some detective, right?"

"Sam Spade. He was a private detective in San Francisco, back in the 1920s," Joe explained. "The book starts off with the appearance of this beautiful woman, Miss Wonderly, in Sam Spade's office. She asks Sam Spade to help find her sister, who ran off with a creepy guy named Floyd Thursby. So Sam Spade's partner, Miles Archer, follows the guy."

"And?"

"A couple of hours later the partner is found shot dead," Joe went on. "Then someone kills Floyd Thursby, and the cops think it was Sam Spade."

"Wait. Let me get this straight," said Sam, holding up a hand. "You mean, the cops think Thursby killed Sam Spade's partner, and that Spade killed Thursby for revenge?"

Joe nodded. "Right. Except that Sam Spade didn't kill anyone. He finds out Miss Wonderly made up the whole story about her sister. Her real name is

Brigid O'Shaughnessy. She's mixed up in the whole thing, but she won't tell Sam Spade how. She just begs him to help her, saying she's afraid she'll be killed next. Spade doesn't trust Brigid, but he decides to help her, anyway. I guess he's kind of in love with her."

"Uh-oh. Sounds like trouble." Sam shook her head, handing the book back to Joe.

"I'll say. And I'm only up to Chapter Three. I haven't even read anything about a Maltese falcon yet, but I'm guessing it has something to do with the murders," Joe said. "The whole thing is pretty creepy so far. I mean, *everyone* seems kind of suspicious, and no one trusts anyone else."

"Makes you kind of glad *we* don't have those problems in Oakdale, doesn't it?" Sam said, grinning.

"Definitely," Joe agreed. He tapped the cover of *The Maltese Falcon*, then dropped the book into his sports bag along with his homework. "I mean, can you imagine guys wearing dark suits and carrying guns lurking around Oakdale?"

"Not really." Sam laughed, and then said in a teasing voice, "But you never can tell. Maybe you'd better start watching your back, Joe."

Joe was fifteen minutes early for basketball practice that afternoon. When he got to the gym, it was empty except for Coach Allen and Damont. Damont sat in the first row, wearing shorts and his practice shirt. He was bent forward, his forearms on his knees and his skin visible through his close-cropped hair.

Coach Allen stood in front of Damont, wearing red sweats. He had a whistle on a cord around his neck. The afternoon sunlight coming through the gym's large windows glistened on the coach's dark-brown skin. The look in his eyes was serious as he spoke.

"Everyone knows that you're a superior player, Damont," said Coach Allen.

"You got *that* right," Damont put in.

The coach ignored Damont's wisecrack. "But," he went on, "you've got to try to work *with* the team more. . . ."

Joe tried not to eavesdrop. He left his towel and water bottle in their usual spot, in a corner next to the bleachers. Then he went to get a basketball from a net bag by the sidelines. As he fished one out, he over-heard more of what the coach was saying to Damont.

"I don't have to tell you how much it would mean to this team to earn another championship banner," Coach Allen went on.

He glanced at the wall between the gym's entrance and the hall that led to the locker room. That was where the Bulldogs's championship banners and trophies were kept.

Joe spotted the last championship banner the basketball team had won—a full seven years earlier. It was made of blue felt, with the year and the words "LEAGUE CHAMPS" in gold. The banner had become worn and stained over time. Looking at it, Joe felt determined to do his part to win a bright *new* banner this season.

"We may be on an early winning streak," said the coach, "but we're going to have to do even better if we want to end the season as champs." He took a deep breath, leveling a serious look at Damont. "Think about passing the ball more, giving the team more of a chance to work together. Take Joe, for instance. His real strength is that he's not afraid to rely on the other players. You could learn from that, Damont. You need to be more of a team player."

Joe tried not to show that he'd heard the coach's remarks. But as he started to dribble the basketball and do layups, he couldn't help but grin. The coach was actually telling Damont to play more like *him!*

Damont was scowling when he joined Joe on the court a few minutes later. "Watch it, Talbot," he said. Damont blew past Joe, knocking him off balance with his shoulder. Then Damont dribbled toward the basket and jumped for the layup. That was when Joe noticed Damont's sneakers. They were brand-new, ultra-high-tech—and almost exactly like Joe's.

"I guess you don't like being outplayed or out-dressed," Joe said under his breath.

Damont's answer was a lightning-fast pass aimed right at Joe's face. "Think fast."

Joe barely managed to deflect the ball. "Hey! We're supposed to be on the same team, remember?"

"Only because I'm stuck with you," Damont scoffed. "Don't think for a second that you'll ever be my equal on the—"

"Damont! I want you and Joe to work on passing until the rest of the team gets here," the coach said.

Joe knew what the coach was really saying: Play

together, not against each other. Damont frowned, but Joe doubted he would challenge the coach. Coach Allen could be tough, but he was fair. Every boy on the team respected him.

For the next ten minutes, Joe and Damont practiced passing. Joe was so busy concentrating on his playing that he didn't see Jimmy Kidd and a few other younger boys arrive. All of a sudden they were there, sitting in the stands with their jackets and backpacks piled around them. Joe had gotten used to seeing Jimmy at practices. Jimmy was only in the fourth grade, but he came after school almost every day to watch Damont.

Apparently, the Bulldogs's winning streak was attracting more fans than usual, thought Joe. Lately, some other boys had been showing up with Jimmy. One of them was Marcus Finch, whose uncle, Travis Del Rio, owned the sports store in town.

Joe's attention strayed from his playing for just half a second, but he nearly missed Damont's next pass. He scrambled, ignoring the taunting look on Damont's face. Then he shot the ball back in a bounce-pass.

Every time Damont passed, he flung the ball full force at Joe. He was obviously trying to provoke Joe, but Joe made himself focus on his own playing. He and Damont didn't stop until they heard the coach's annoyed voice.

"You two are late," the coach said.

Joe wiped the sweat from his forehead. Two of his teammates, Hank and Drew, were just jogging into the gym. They both looked sheepish.

"Sorry, Coach," Hank said. "Some of the guys were—"

"Hank, where are your protective pads?" the coach cut in. "You can't risk bruising your knee again." He frowned as a handful of players trickled in behind Hank and Drew. "Haven't you boys ever heard of sweat bands? And where are your water bottles? Just because we've won a few games doesn't mean we can start slacking off."

"We're *not!*" Hank insisted. "I left my pads in my locker, but now they're not there."

"I couldn't find my stuff, either," said another player. "That's why I'm late. I was looking all over for it."

Coach Allen's frown deepened. "Enough excuses. You boys had better get yourselves in gear. Our next game is against the Jefferson Bobcats. Do I have to remind you they were regional champs last year? If we don't get organized, we won't stand a chance against them."

Drew looked helplessly at the other players. "But, Coach, we really couldn't—"

"No buts," Coach Allen said firmly. "I want everyone in two lines for running drills. Now."

Joe wasn't about to question the coach. For the next half-hour, he and the rest of the team did running, dribbling, passing, layup, and jump-shot drills. Joe forgot all about the players' remarks about missing equipment—until they took a break.

He was in the middle of taking a long drink from his sports bottle when he saw Hank and Drew approach the coach.

"Uh . . . Coach? About all that stuff we couldn't find . . ." Hank began. "We were just in the locker room, and . . ." He and Drew looked uncomfortably at each other. "Well, could you come take a look?"

Coach Allen glanced back and forth between the two players, then nodded. "All right."

Joe was so curious that he followed the coach, Hank, and Drew into the locker room. They went to the end of the row of lockers. Between the last locker and the wall was a narrow gap. Drew reached into it and pulled out a knee pad.

"What the . . . ?" Bending down, the coach pulled out another knee pad from the narrow gap. Several water bottles and sweat bands tumbled out after it.

"Someone hid the equipment," Hank said. "They stuffed it in here so we couldn't find it."

Joe could hardly believe his eyes. "You mean someone did that on purpose?" he asked. "But who? And why?"

Chapter Three

"Exshellent shtew, as ushual, Ellen!" Wishbone trotted to the back door, holding a meaty soup bone in his mouth. "But shnack time ish over, and I'm ready for adventhure! I've got places to shmell . . . bones to bury . . . dogs to see!" Wishbone scratched at the door, then glanced up at Ellen. *"Hellooo!* Can you let me out now? Pleashe?"

"What's the hurry, Wishbone?" Ellen asked. She placed the lid on the stew pot, then patted Wishbone before opening the door. "Can't wait to go bury that bone, eh?"

"You got it! But that's not all. You see, I was hoping to run into a certain Yorkshire terrier. . . ."

Romping with Yorkie the evening before had been lots of fun. First, they had played tug-of-war with an old sock they'd found in the alley next to Pepper Pete's. Then they'd gone to Jackson Park. It was one of Wishbone's favorite places to roam, and Yorkie seemed to love it as much as he did.

She had been eager to play all Wishbone's favorite

games. They'd rolled joyfully in the leaves together. When Wishbone had spotted some squirrels hiding acorns, Yorkie had raced after them with the same enthusiasm as Wishbone, her pink tongue hanging out with glee. Even before Wishbone showed her his favorite digging spots among the tree roots, she seemed to know exactly where they were.

What a dog! She was cute and fun-loving. Wishbone didn't know much about her, but he felt he and Yorkie understood each other in a way he'd never felt with other dogs. Sure, Wishbone had other pals in the neighborhood. But with Yorkie it was different. Was it because she was a terrier, too? Wishbone didn't know. But he *did* know he couldn't wait to play with Yorkie again.

"See you later, Ellen!" Wishbone leaped outside, then ran to the front yard. "Yorkie . . . Oh, *Yor*-kie!"

He turned his head when he heard a rustling in the bushes across the street. "Shiny white fur, wet nose . . . It's Yorkie, all right!"

As Yorkie appeared from among the leaves, Wishbone carefully crossed the street and ran over to her. He dropped his bone in front of her and barked his most enthusiastic hello.

"Am I glad to see you! Want to play? I brought you a bone."

Yorkie pounced on the bone, her tail wagging. She gnawed off the meat, then looked at Wishbone with eyes that begged for more.

"That's all I've got. But the fun's not over yet! I know the perfect place to bury that."

Wishbone trotted over to the garden of the

Talbots' next-door neighbor, Wanda Gilmore. He pawed at the soft earth of her flower beds.

"Some of my best bones are here already. I'll show you. Call it my way of saying 'Welcome to the neighborhood!'"

Yorkie went to work alongside him, digging with gusto. Glancing over at her, Wishbone saw it again—the inviting look in her eyes that told him Yorkie understood what a special spot this was to him. It made Wishbone yelp with pure pleasure.

"I knew you would like it here!"

Of course, Yorkie *was* something of a mystery. Wishbone hardly knew a thing about her. That made her even more mysterious.

"I see you're not wearing tags. Don't you have a family, Yorkie?"

If she did, Yorkie wasn't saying. She just kept digging.

Wishbone crouched over on his front paws and looked up into her big eyes. "Okay, so you don't want to talk about your family. Well, then, how do you like Oakdale? Are you planning to stay long?"

Again, no answer. Before Wishbone could ask anything else, he heard a familiar whistle from the street. Dan Bloodgood, the local mail carrier, was just stepping away from his mail cart with a handful of letters. Wishbone had had his share of run-ins with mail carriers in the past, but Dan was different. There was something almost . . . canine about him.

"Hi, Wishbone," Dan called in a friendly voice. "I see you've got company today."

"You bet!" Wishbone barked a greeting. "This is

Yorkie, and she's . . ." Wishbone turned to where Yorkie had been digging. All he saw was a dug-up hole. "She's gone!"

"Looks like your company's got company." Dan nodded toward Wanda's side yard, where Yorkie now stood. She was nose to nose with Jimmy Kidd's chihuahua, Dinky, and a sleek Doberman that Wishbone recognized from around the neighborhood. Dinky held a good-sized stick in his mouth, and Yorkie was sniffing it from end to end.

"Nice stick, Dinky. But, hey, Yorkie!" Wishbone picked up his bone, which Yorkie had dropped. "Don't you want to finish digging—"

"Wishbone!" Wanda's shrill voice came from her front door. "You've been at my flower beds again!"

Wanda was a wonderful person, and a terrific gardener. But she could be overly picky about her flower beds. Couldn't she see the soft earth there was perfect for digging? No dog could resist it!

"I can explain, Wanda. It's all part of my 'Welcome to the neighborhood!' campaign." Wishbone held up his bone to show her. "My friend Yorkie, here, is new in town and . . . Hey, Yorkie! Where are you going?"

Yorkie was trotting into the bushes at the edge of Wanda's yard—right behind Dinky and the Doberman.

Wishbone could hardly believe his eyes. "You're leaving? Just like that? Without even a farewell bark? Yorkie, wait!"

The little white terrier didn't even look back.

With a sigh, Wishbone sat back on his haunches—then yelped. Wanda was marching toward him, an angry frown on her face.

"Like I said, I can explain . . . later! Right now I've got to do what any self-respecting dog would—*run!*"

Wishbone didn't stop running until he reached Sequoyah Middle School. Maybe he couldn't play with Yorkie *or* dig in Wanda's garden. But he *could* cheer on his best pal at basketball practice.

A boy opened the school's front door on his way out, and Wishbone darted inside and trotted to the gym. Wishbone saw Billy Kidd, Marcus Finch, and a few other boys sitting in the bleachers, but the court was empty. Wishbone didn't find the players until he pushed through the double doors leading to the locker room.

"Joe, old pal, old buddy! It sure is good to see a friendly face." Tail wagging, Wishbone trotted over to the benches where Joe, his teammates, and Coach Allen were gathered. The little dog stopped short when he saw the serious expressions on the boys' faces. "What's wrong? Did someone pass a new leash law?"

"Hi, Wishbone," Joe said, scratching Wishbone behind the ears. "What have you been up to?"

"Don't listen to a word Wanda says! Yorkie and I had important work in her garden, and . . ."

Wishbone stopped when he realized no one was listening. The boys seemed to have other things on their minds.

"I still can't believe someone hid our equipment," said one of Joe's teammates, whose name Wishbone knew was Drew.

Wishbone's ears perked up. "Hid? You mean, *on purpose?* Who would do that?"

As the boys kept talking, Wishbone realized there had been big trouble at practice.

"Wow! Major intrigue, right here in Oakdale. Well, if there's one thing I love, it's a mystery! Never fear, guys. Wishbone is on the case. *I'll* find that missing equipment!"

Nose to the ground, Wishbone began a tour of the locker room. He sniffed a sweaty T-shirt that dangled from an open locker. "Hmm . . . I wouldn't mind a few of these for my personal collection. And this . . ." He stopped at the corner of a bench to sniff at a scrap of blue fabric caught between the boards. "This looks like part of the championship banner. But why is there just a tiny piece of it?

"Oh, Joe!" Wishbone barked, pawing at the scrap of felt. "Take a look over here. This could be a clue!"

"What's your dog's problem, Talbot?" Damont scoffed.

"What have you got there, boy?" Joe came over to Wishbone and crouched down. "What's this?" he said, looking at the scrap of felt. "Hey, isn't this a piece of—"

"The championship banner," Coach Allen finished. He pulled the fabric free of the boards and frowned down at it. Without saying a word, he walked quickly from the locker room.

When the coach returned a moment later, Wishbone saw that the frown on his face was even deeper.

"The banner is gone," Coach Allen announced.

"So I was right. This *is* an important clue!" Wishbone wagged his tail and looked up at Joe. "Well, Joe, what do you think it means?"

The boys and Coach Allen stared silently at one another. Hank frowned and said, "This is too weird. Do you think whoever hid the equipment stashed the banner, too?"

For the next few minutes, Wishbone, Joe, and the other members of the team searched the locker room. Wishbone sniffed in every corner, but the rest of the blue-felt banner was nowhere to be found.

"Where could it be?" Joe wondered, leaning against the lockers with a sigh. "I saw the banner when I got to practice. It was hanging right on the wall, where it always is. Why would anyone take it?"

"No one's even been here except us," Drew pointed out.

The boys looked around suspiciously at one another. Wishbone sensed a sudden change in the atmosphere. It was as if they'd smelled a cat among them.

"Listen, I don't want you boys worrying about the banner. We've got to stay focused on our playing," said Coach Allen. "Now that we've got our equipment back, let's get back to practice. I want everyone out on the court in five minutes."

As the boys left the locker room to return to the gym, Wishbone tagged along beside Joe. Joe stopped at the bleachers and took a drink from his water bottle. Jimmy Kidd and a handful of other youngsters were still sitting there. Jimmy was talking, and the others were listening intently.

"So then Damont played a game of one-on-one with Michael Jordan," Jimmy was saying.

"The Michael Jordan?" asked a red-haired boy. "Of the Chicago Bulls? No way!"

"Hi, guys," said Joe.

The boys didn't even look at him.

"It's the truth!" Jimmy insisted. "Michael told Damont the Bulls are interested in recruiting him."

Wishbone noticed Joe smiling and shaking his head from side to side. Wishbone put his front paws on the bleachers and barked. "Talk about a tall tale! Are you always this good at making up stories, Jimmy?"

Seeing Wishbone, Marcus turned and said, "Hi, Joe. Hi, Wishbone!"

Marcus was a great kid. He loved to collect things—a hobby Wishbone heartily approved of. And he always had time to play. Taking off his white Oakdale Sports & Games cap, Marcus held it out to Wishbone for a game of tug-of-war.

"Here's a kid who knows how to play!" Wishbone gave a playful growl and grabbed the cap with his teeth. "But, serioushly, you boys didn't 'appen to see anyone thuspishious with sports bottles and safety pads and stuff lurking in the locker room, did you?"

"Did any of you guys see anything weird today?" Joe asked. "Maybe someone with sports equipment hanging around in the locker room?"

Wishbone looked up at Joe. "Didn't I jusht ask that?"

"Or maybe someone who's not on the team coming out of the locker room?" Joe added.

The boys looked at one another and shook their heads. "We were watching practice. I didn't see anything else," said Marcus. "Why? What happened?"

"There'sh a thief afoot, that'sh what!" Wishbone gave an extra shake to Marcus's cap. "He's taken off with the championship banner."

"Someone hid our equipment," Joe explained. "We found it, though. But our most recent championship banner is missing. Have any of you seen it?"

"Nope. No way," Jimmy said quickly. Too quickly, in Wishbone's opinion. He seemed nervous all of a sudden. "Why would *we* know about any equipment, *or* some dumb banner?"

Wishbone recognized the uneasy look in Jimmy's eyes. Jimmy looked the same way Wishbone felt when Wanda caught him digging in her garden.

Jimmy glanced at Damont, who was practicing shots from mid-court with a few other players. "Well, I've gotta go. See you," Jimmy said. He grabbed his backpack and jacket and scrambled from the bleachers. Then he was gone.

"What was *that* all about?" Joe wondered aloud. "Jimmy always stays for practice, so why is he leaving before it is even over?"

"Anyone who makth such a sspeedy getaway definitely sshould *not* be trusted. Justh ask Wanda!" Wishbone dropped the cap and barked up at Joe. "Makes you wonder what Jimmy is up to, doesn't it?"

Chapter Four

"Jimmy acted strangely when I asked him about the missing equipment," Joe said to Sam and David as they walked to school Thursday morning.

Joe had called Sam and David and asked them to meet him at his house. He had quickly brought them up to speed on his situation.

"*And* don't forget the felt banner." Wishbone trotted lightly along the sidewalk, sniffing the fresh, crisp, dewey air. He had considered taking a morning nap on the living room sofa. But when Sam and David had arrived to walk to school with Joe, Wishbone had decided to go along. Now he was doubly glad of his decision. This way he got to spend time with his close friends *and* help them solve the mystery of the hidden equipment and missing championship banner.

"Do you think Jimmy hid the equipment?" Sam asked.

"He's just a little kid," David said. "Why would he do that?"

Joe shrugged. "I've been thinking. . . . Maybe Jimmy saw *Damont* do something. Damont and I both got to practice early yesterday. And neither of us had any equipment taken—"

"It's possible you or Damont hid everyone *else's* stuff," Sam finished. "Well, we know it wasn't *you.*"

"No way!" Wishbone barked his agreement.

"That leaves Damont," said David.

"I don't know . . ." Sam said, and she bit her lip. "Why would he hide his own teammates' stuff?"

"To make them look bad?" David guessed. "Most of the time Damont acts as if he doesn't care a bit about the rest of the team. All he cares about is how good *he* looks."

Joe nodded. "Jimmy worships Damont. If Damont *did* hide the equipment, Jimmy would never tell on him. And, Damont would get away with it."

"Wow! An unsolved mystery. I *love* mysteries!" Wishbone's paws tapped lightly against the pavement as he trotted along.

"The worst thing is, now *everyone* is wondering who on the team could be guilty," Joe went on. "You should have seen the guys during team play—everyone looking sideways at everyone else. It's almost as bad as what's going on among the characters in *The Maltese Falcon.*"

Wishbone's ears perked up. *The Maltese Falcon* was one of his very favorite mysteries—though he would have preferred a story about a Maltese *dog*. "If I remember the story right," Wishbone recalled, "Detective Sam Spade was surrounded by untrustworthy people, all eagerly looking for the same thing."

"Did you find out anything about a falcon yet?" Sam asked.

"Yes," Joe told her. He then brought David up to date on what he told Sam earlier about *The Maltese Falcon*. "Besides murder, it turns out that there's a priceless gold statue of a falcon, covered with precious jewels. It was covered with black paint to hide the jewels. A bunch of different people are trying to find it, but so far no one has. They all seem ready to lie and cheat to get their hands on the falcon. Sam Spade doesn't trust any of them."

"What about that woman, the one Sam Spade is in love with?" Sam asked.

"Brigid O'Shaughnessy," Joe said. "She keeps lying to him, too. She won't say what she knows about the falcon. All she tells him is that she's afraid the other people who want the statue will kill her in order to get it. Two different guys have already tried to make Sam Spade turn against Brigid and help them get the falcon. Spade pretends he might make a deal—that he's only looking out for himself—but he keeps protecting Brigid."

"That no-good feline has him wrapped around her little paw! Ah, well . . . I guess some slobbery hounds will do anything for love." Wishbone shook his head, then looked around curiously. "By the way, has anyone seen Yorkie?"

"Sounds like it's every man for himself," David commented. "That has to be uncomfortable for everyone—being suspicious of other people all the time. Joe, it's not *that* bad on the team, is it?"

Joe shook his head. "Things are just a little uneasy,

that's all," he said. "I'm probably overreacting. But anyway, I hope that from now on the only trouble I learn about is in *The Maltese Falcon*."

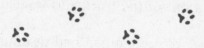

Wishbone paused when Joe, Sam, and David came to the school. The spongy grass felt wonderful under his paws. A thousand different smells called out for him to investigate.

"See you guys later. I'm outta here!" Wishbone barked a good-bye, and then he was off.

His first stop was a large, leafy oak tree. As he sniffed at the roots, Wishbone picked up the scents of several other dogs. It wasn't long before he heard another pair of paws scratching at the earth.

"Oh, good, company!" He stopped in mid-sniff when he saw who it was. "Yorkie!"

As she came around the tree trunk, the terrier's tail was wagging, her eyes bright. Wishbone sniffed tentatively at her silky tail.

"Uh . . . Yorkie? You probably didn't *mean* to hurt my feelings in Wanda's garden yesterday. But . . . well, why did you drop me like a worn-out squeaky toy?"

Yorkie grabbed a stick in her mouth. Wishbone could tell she was ready to play. Wishbone wanted to play, too. But he couldn't just ignore what had happened.

"I thought you were my friend, Yorkie, my soul mate." Wishbone sat down and gazed at her with sincerity. "But maybe you're just a fair-weather—"

A movement at the edge of the park suddenly

caught Wishbone's attention. A truck was pulling up to the curb. Printed on its side were the words OAKDALE ANIMAL CONTROL. A woman with curly brown hair and dark skin got out of the truck and walked toward the oak tree.

"Uh-oh." Wishbone had had dealings with Officer Garcia in the past. She was just as stiff and no-nonsense as the brown uniform and cap she wore. "This could be trouble, Yorkie. I think she just noticed you don't have tags!"

As Officer Garcia came closer, she reached a hand in Yorkie's direction. "Come on, now," she said. "Don't make this harder than it has to be."

Yorkie turned to Wishbone with helpless eyes. He couldn't think of deserting her. "Maybe you did leave me . . . uh . . . holding the bone in Wanda's garden. But *no* dog deserves the dog pound." Wishbone barked and ran into the bushes. "I'll help you hide, Yorkie. Come on!"

Yorkie yapped and charged into the bushes after him, with the animal-control officer only a few steps behind.

"All strays must be caught," muttered Officer Garcia. "It's for the safety of the public!"

"We dogs are part of the public, too!" Wishbone gave an upset bark. "And having you around does *not* make me feel safe!"

Wishbone dodged into a thick ring of azalea bushes. Was Yorkie still all right? His heart pounded until he saw the terrier burst through the branches behind him, panting. Her eyes were still fearful, but they held a glimmer of excitement, too.

"'Atta girl, Yorkie! We can still escape the clutches of Officer Garcia!"

Wishbone searched for low-lying thick branches that Officer Garcia couldn't go through. He and Yorkie scampered from one hedge to another. At last, they no longer heard the animal-control officer's footsteps plodding behind them.

"Yippee!" Wishbone dropped down and rolled in the leaves. He batted at a burr with his paw, while Yorkie pounced on his tail. Playing with her, Wishbone was sure what had happened the day before was simply a mistake.

This is the real Yorkie, he thought. *A fun, brave terrier who sticks by her pal.*

"You *do* stick by me, don't you, Yorkie?"

Yorkie rolled in the leaves without answering.

Chapter Five

Joe was glad to see that everyone on the team arrived at practice on time Thursday afternoon. The first thing the coach did was separate them into two practice teams. After what had happened the day before, Joe had a feeling they would all be watching one another carefully.

Stay on your toes, he told himself. *Defense will probably be hot today.* Even though he felt his game was strong, he didn't want to be caught off guard.

At the tipoff, the center tapped the ball to Joe. Joe dribbled downcourt, keeping his eyes on the defensive players as he angled toward the basket. The ball felt just right against his palm, his sneakers solid on the floor. Joe could sense, rather than see, exactly where each of his teammates was. It was one of those days when everything felt perfectly in sync.

The defensive guard flicked a hand out, trying to steal the ball. Joe jumped back and dribbled the ball out of reach.

"Focus, Hank! You should have been all over Joe!"

Coach Allen called out. "I want to see a strong zone defense!"

Hank grimaced, shaking first one sneaker, then the other. "It's my feet. They're hot."

"Is that the best excuse you can come up with?" Damont muttered. He spun around the other team's defense, opening himself up for the pass.

Joe wasn't about to miss his chance. He sent the ball flying toward Damont. Damont started to reach out—then grimaced and looked down at his sneakers. Joe couldn't believe it when the ball went out of bounds.

So much for everything being in sync, he thought with a sigh.

"That was sloppy, Damont," called the coach. "You were right there. What happened?"

"Something's wrong!" Damont hopped from foot to foot. "My feet feel like someone put hot chili peppers on them!"

Looking around, Joe saw some of the other guys shaking their feet and tugging at their laces. Coach Allen told them to keep playing, but Joe's teammates couldn't seem to keep their minds on the game. Half a dozen boys complained of burning and itching feet. After a while, the coach blew his whistle and told them to take a break.

Joe grabbed his towel from its usual spot next to the bleachers, then sat down on the lowest bench. A few rows behind him, Jimmy, Marcus, and a handful of other fourth-graders watched with interest.

"Do you boys expect me to believe every single one of you has suddenly been stricken with a serious case of athlete's foot?" Coach Allen asked.

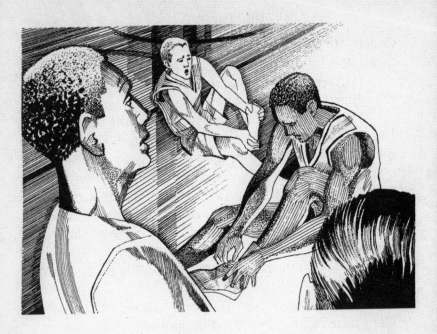

"All I know is that I can't take the pain anymore!" said Hank.

Murmurs of agreement came from several teammates. Damont and some other boys unlaced their sneakers, removed their socks, and squirted water over their feet.

What's going on? wondered Joe. His own feet felt fine, but a lot of the guys were obviously having serious problems.

"Hey!" said Damont, frowning into his sneakers. "There's some kind of powder in here that I did not put in!"

"There's some in mine, too," said Hank. He lifted his sneakers for a closer look, then started sneezing out of control.

Coach Allen took one of Hank's sneakers and

rubbed some of the powder on his fingers. "Itching powder," he said.

No way. He can't be serious, thought Joe. But one look at the sneezing, irritated faces of his teammates and Joe knew it was true.

The prankster had struck again.

"First someone hides equipment, then the banner, and now this," said Joe, thinking out loud. "What's going on?"

"That's what *I'd* like to know," Coach Allen said, frowning. "I want everyone with itching powder to go wash it off. Then we're going to sit down and figure this thing out."

Half a dozen guys, including Damont and Hank, bolted for the locker room. Joe sat on the bleachers with the rest of the team. Everyone looked uncomfortable. Whispers buzzed back and forth. Even Marcus, Jimmy, and the other fourth-graders had stopped joking around and were watching quietly.

Once the team members were all reassembled, Coach Allen paced the floor in front of them. "How could this have happened?" he asked, a serious look on his face. "Any ideas?"

Damont looked at his teammates and shrugged. "All my practice stuff was in the locker room. Anyone could have gone in there before practice and put the powder in my sneakers."

"No locks?" asked the coach.

Hank shook his head. "I never use one. Nobody does. We've never had any trouble before. My stuff was in the locker room last night, too."

"So was mine," Drew spoke up.

43

The coach questioned each player in turn. Every single boy who had left his sneakers in the locker room had wound up with itching powder in them. At least, it seemed that way—until it was Joe's turn to respond.

"Were your sneakers in the locker room last night?" asked Coach Allen.

"Yes," Joe said, "but my feet are fine."

The coach frowned. "Are you sure?"

Joe nodded, but he took off his sneakers to check them, anyway. "Nothing," he said, showing them to the coach. "No powder."

"That's weird," said Hank. "Why would everyone who left their sneakers in their lockers last night have itching powder in them, but not you?"

"I don't know," Joe said. He had been wondering the same thing, but he hadn't come up with an answer that made sense.

"I think *I* know," Damont said. He turned to Joe with a look that made Joe feel suddenly ill at ease. "Maybe it's because *Joe* did it."

"What! You can't be serious!" Joe exclaimed. "I didn't do anything."

"I think *you* put that itching powder in everyone's sneakers," said Damont.

That same afternoon, Wishbone ran happily from the woods in Jackson Park into the grassy field behind the school. He turned to his new friend. "Hey, Yorkie, come with me!"

Yorkie raced from the woods, a big smile on her

face. She and Wishbone had been romping ever since they'd escaped from the animal-control officer. They had sniffed around, dug up bones, and chased things. It was so much fun that Wishbone was more sure than ever that he and Yorkie were meant for each other.

"Hi, Dinky! Hi, guys." Wishbone wagged his tail as a handful of dogs came out of the woods behind Yorkie.

A large retriever dragged a dirty old sock onto the field and dropped it on the grass next to Yorkie. Yorkie grabbed the sock in her mouth—only to drop it again when Dinky appeared with a dirt-covered bone.

"Pretty impressive, Dinky. But I think I can do even better. Come with me, Yorkie!" Wishbone ran toward some bushes at the edge of the woods. Sunlight glinted off something shiny and metallic on the ground. "Hey, look at this! A tin box."

Wishbone pawed at the box, and a fine white powder spilled from a hole at one end of it. Yorkie's excited bark made Wishbone so happy he rolled over, rubbing his back and head in the powder-covered dirt.

"You should try this, Yorkie. It feels—" A powerful sneeze cut off Wishbone's next words. The Jack Russell terrier jumped up, yelping and sneezing. All of a sudden, his whole back was itchy. His nose felt as if it were on fire.

"Ouch!Ouch!Ouch!Ouch!" Wishbone rolled in the grass, trying to rub off the awful feeling. Nothing helped. The only thing he could do was yelp with pain. *"Heeeellllp!"*

45

"Let's call it a day," said Coach Allen. "Those of you who had itching powder in your sneakers, I want you to get your shoes cleaned up. And I want *all* of you to be ready to make up for lost time tomorrow. We concentrate on basketball tomorrow. And, no more accusations unless you have proof."

As Joe grabbed his towel and his sports bottle, he sensed the eyes of his teammates staring at him. It made him feel terrible. How could they misjudge him this way? He wanted to tell them again, *I didn't do anything!* But he knew that wouldn't help.

"This is all your fault, Talbot," Damont muttered, glaring at Joe.

"That's for sure," Jimmy spoke up from the bleachers.

"That's enough," the coach called out sternly. "I repeat once again, I won't have my players accusing one another. And I'll thank you boys in the peanut gallery to stay out of this."

Great, Joe thought, letting out a sigh. *Even a ten-year-old kid suspects me.*

He thought of Wishbone. Wishbone could usually make him feel better by licking his hand, or gazing up at him with those understanding eyes, at exactly the right moment. But Joe's pal wasn't there.

Jimmy scrambled down the bleachers to his cousin and said, "No one ever should have messed with *your* sneakers, Damont. That was a big mistake. . . ." He was trying hard to impress Damont, but Damont barely looked at him.

For the first time ever, Joe couldn't wait to get away from practice. He pushed quickly through the locker room doors, then paused when he heard barking. It was loud and frantic—and it sounded *awfully* familiar.

"Wishbone?" Picking up his pace, Joe followed the noise. Not bothering to change his clothes, he hurried to the back door of the locker room, which was used to get out to the field for football and soccer games. The metal door was ajar, and the barking came from right outside.

Joe pushed the door fully open and stepped outside. There, at the edge of the field, was Wishbone, howling and jumping around like crazy.

"It is you! What's the matter, boy?" Joe asked with great concern.

Joe ran over to Wishbone, stroking his nose and trying to calm him down. He had never seen Wishbone so worked up before.

"What is it?" he asked. "What's that white stuff all over your fur?"

Just then, Joe spotted a metal tin in the dirt near Wishbone.

He picked it up, then frowned when he read the label aloud: "Itching powder."

Joe quickly dropped the box. "Yikes!" His fingertips felt as if they were burning. "This stuff really *does* sting," he said, rubbing the powder off on his shorts.

Using his sports bottle and towel, he started to clean the powder off Wishbone.

"Okay, calm down, Wishbone. You'll feel better in a minute. . . ."

Joe's mind was racing. Whoever put the powder in everyone's sneakers must have ditched it under the bushes, he realized. Maybe that is why the door was open. . . .

"Check it out." Damont's voice broke into Joe's thoughts. Damont was standing behind him and Wishbone, Joe saw. Some of the other basketball team members were just outside the locker room doorway. They must have heard Wishbone barking also.

"Looks like Talbot's dog dug up the evidence," Damont continued. "You should have found a better hiding place for that itching powder, Joe."

Joe's mouth dropped open. "I didn't hide the powder, Damont, and I didn't do anything!"

Damont leveled a cool look at Wishbone and said, "Then why is your dog covered with itching powder?"

Wishbone barked in Damont's direction. He seemed so earnest and forceful that Joe almost had the impression Wishbone was trying to say something to Damont.

"I don't know. Wishbone digs up stuff all the time," Joe said. He couldn't believe how twisted around the entire situation had gotten. "Come on, guys! You know me better. You've got to believe me."

Joe gazed past Damont at his other teammates. He waited for them to say they believed him, that they knew he would never do anything so sneaky and mean.

Instead, they said nothing. . . .

Chapter Six

"Joe didn't do it, I tell you!" Wishbone rose up on his hind legs and barked. Now that Joe had washed that awful powder off him, he finally found his voice again. "My pal Joe would *never* resort to foul play! Just ask my canine buddies here. They'll guarantee that Joe is an honest guy."

Wishbone looked around for Yorkie and the other dogs, but they were gone.

"Whoops!" he said. "Well, I guess it *is* getting close to kibble time. You boys will have to believe *me*, then." Wishbone rubbed up against Joe, his tail wagging. "Joe is absolutely above suspicion. Case closed."

"If you *didn't* leave that itching powder out here, then who *did?*" asked Damont.

"I don't have a clue—any more than you do or anyone else does, for that matter," said Joe.

Now that Wishbone was standing among Joe's teammates, he understood why Joe was reminded of *The Maltese Falcon*. The boys really were distrustful, just like the characters in Dashiell Hammett's mystery. What Wishbone *didn't* understand was why anyone would suspect his boy. The awkward situation Joe found himself in made Wishbone more determined than ever to get to the bottom of who was playing the pranks.

"If anyone can find out who left that itching powder here, I can!" Wishbone put his nose to the ground—careful to avoid the powdery patch. "I can sniff out clues as well as any detective . . . even one so talented as Sam Spade. I've got the nose for it, after all."

Wishbone had taken only a few steps when Coach Allen came through the locker room doorway. "What's going on out here?" the coach asked. "What was all that barking?"

"Try getting a whiff of this stuff and see how *you* like it." Wishbone carefully knocked the empty tin across the grass with his paw.

"Wishbone found the itching powder," Joe said.

"You mean, he got covered in the powder and tipped us off to your hiding place," Damont muttered.

"Enough." The coach crossed his arms over his chest and looked seriously at Joe and Damont. "These pranks are no joke, boys. We're on a real winning streak—maybe on our way to achieving the league championship. I don't understand why *anyone* would put that chance at risk," he said. "But what really disturbs me is that you've started blaming one another."

"You tell 'em, Coach!" Wishbone trotted over to Coach Allen, his head held high.

The coach eyed Wishbone and gave a wry smile.

"One little powder-covered dog is hardly concrete proof of guilt," the coach went on. "You boys should know that."

"Excuse me, sir." Wishbone glanced up at the coach. "I believe what you meant to say was one *cute* powder-covered dog. . . ."

"But let me make one thing perfectly clear." Coach Allen looked each boy directly in the eye before continuing. "If I find out for sure that *any* player was behind these pranks—Joe or anyone else—that boy will be suspended from the team."

"This guy means business. But, hey, it sounds fair to me—especially since we know you didn't do anything, Joe."

Wishbone wagged his tail, but his smile faltered when he saw the stony looks on the faces of Joe's teammates.

"So . . . uh . . . there's nothing to worry about. Right?" Wishbone said, not so sure after all.

A half-hour later, Joe sat on a bench in the locker room. Wishbone sat on the floor beside him. The other boys had left, but Joe stayed behind, lost in thought.

"How could this have happened, Wishbone?" Joe said. "Damont has the other guys thinking I'm trying to foul up their playing. What a mess."

With a sigh, Joe reached down to pat Wishbone. Wishbone looked up at him with such warmth that Joe had the feeling the terrier understood what he was saying.

"I guess now I know how Sam Spade felt when the cops falsely suspected him of killing someone," Joe went on. "The trouble is, I don't have any idea how to convince everyone I am innocent."

Joe changed clothes and threw his basketball sneakers and practice clothes into his sports bag. "Well, we might as well get going, boy. Mom will start to worry if we're not home soon for dinner."

Joe began to zip up his bag, then stopped when Wishbone poked his nose inside.

"No playing around, boy," Joe said. He chuckled as his dog closed his mouth around something. "We've got to . . ."

Joe's voice trailed off when he saw what was clamped in Wishbone's mouth. It was his dad's copy of *The Maltese Falcon*. Joe took the book from Wishbone and tapped the cover, thinking.

"Hmm . . . If Sam Spade can figure out the mystery of the missing Maltese falcon *and* solve a couple of murders, I ought to be able to figure out who's behind the pranks here at Sequoyah. . . ."

Wishbone barked once, trotted to the outside door, and barked again. If Joe hadn't known better, he would almost have thought Wishbone had fished out the book on purpose. But of course that was impossible.

Joe felt a fresh burst of energy. He wasn't about to break into people's houses or go through their things, the way Sam Spade did. But there had to be *something* he could do to find out who the prankster was.

One of the things that impressed Joe about Sam Spade was his incredible eye for detail. *He never misses a clue*, thought Joe. *And neither will I.*

Joe finished zipping up his bag and slung it over his shoulder, then went out the back door to the field. Wishbone bounded past him, racing toward the bushes where he'd found the tin of itching powder.

"How'd you know where we were going, Wishbone? Just keep clear of that itching powder!" Joe called out.

Wishbone stopped a few feet from the tin and barked until Joe caught up with him. *What now?* Joe thought. He picked up the tin, then sighed. *What am I supposed to do, check it for prints?*

Joe began to look slowly around the bush where he'd found the tin of itching powder. He wasn't sure what he expected to find. Maybe whoever had left the tin there had dropped something? Or left some footprints?

Joe bent to examine the earth beneath the bush. There were some scratch marks, but Joe had a feeling Wishbone had made them, not a person. He didn't see any footprints. There *was* an old sock a few feet away. It was caked with dirt and dried leaves and looked as if it had been there for ages. Joe doubted it belonged to the prankster.

Shading his eyes from the late-afternoon sun, Joe scanned the area. He saw evergreens, dried leaves, and empty bottles—nothing suspicious.

He was about to give up when he spotted something dark among the bushes to the right.

Joe took a step toward the dark shape, then stopped when Wishbone suddenly began to bark. Looking left, Joe saw that the terrier was facing the woods, his body stiff.

"What is it, boy?" Joe asked.

He peered into the woods—then jumped when he caught a flash of movement. Someone was there!

"Hey! Stop!" Joe called.

All he saw was a flash of white as the person took off, heading deeper into the woods.

"Wait!" Joe ran after the figure.

Wishbone was barking behind him, but Joe kept his attention on the person up ahead. The evergreen trees were so thick that Joe couldn't really see who it was. But snapping branches and rustling leaves told him he was hot on the person's trail.

"I'm right behind you," he muttered. Branches whipped at his face, but he didn't slow down. Gritting his teeth, Joe poured on more speed. He could hear the person more clearly now. It sounded as if whoever it was had made it to just beyond the clump of bushes ahead of Joe. Joe angled around them. *Just a few more yards and—*

Joe's foot caught on something, throwing him off balance. "Ahhhh!"

He flew forward at top speed. In one dizzying glance, he saw branches and leaves fly past him. As he went down, he spotted a large, jagged rock sticking out of the ground. He was falling so quickly, it looked as if the rock was flying up at him. In a second, Joe realized, he would hit the rock straight on, with his head.

Chapter Seven

"Joe!" Wishbone yelped when he saw Joe's head flying toward a sharp boulder. "Look out!"

At the last second, Joe threw his hands out to break his fall. He twisted to the side, hitting the ground with a thud.

"Youch! Are you all right, buddy?" Wishbone raced over to Joe and began to lick his face. "Two eyes, nose, ears . . . No cuts, and all the major features are still in place. Nice save, Joe!"

With a groan, Joe pushed himself to a sitting position. "Don't worry, I'm okay, Wishbone," he said. Joe brushed some dried leaves from his hands, then got to his feet and looked around. "I can't believe this. I let that person get away, and I never even got a good look at whoever it was."

"That scoundrel!" Wishbone trotted in the direction the person had taken. "If I ever find out who— Whoa!"

Wishbone's paws caught on something and he stumbled to the ground. When he got back up on all fours, Wishbone saw that he hadn't tripped over a vine or a rock. A *string* was stretched between two trees, just below his chest. "This was no accident, Joe." Wishbone grabbed the string in his mouth and growled. "Look!"

"What's that?" Joe bent down and fingered the string, frowning. "Someone *tied* that string there," he said. "Whoever it was tripped me on purpose!"

"Then he's a double scoundrel!" Wishbone tugged on the string until it broke. Then he rolled over on the ground, tangling himself in the stuff. "Well, I'm not going to take this lying down—after I'm finished playing with this, that is."

Wishbone rolled into the branches of an evergreen. All of a sudden something white dropped over his muzzle. Wishbone tried to roll away from it, but the thing covered his eyes and nose.

"Joe, help!"

"It's a cap," Joe murmured.

"A cap?" Wishbone was relieved when Joe uncovered his eyes and he could see again.

"'Oakdale Sports and Games.'" Joe read the words printed on the cap in green letters. "I saw something white when the person took off. Whoever it was must have been wearing *this!*"

"Good deduction, Joe. Sam Spade couldn't have done any better!" Wishbone sat up and wagged his tail—until he saw how serious Joe looked. "What's wrong? This is a clue. That's good, right?"

"Travis Del Rio gives these out to some customers who buy at his store," Joe said. "Dozens of people have them. What am I supposed to do, search them all?"

"I see what you mean."

Wishbone followed along as Joe made his way back through the woods. When they got to the field, Wishbone expected Joe to start toward home. Instead, Joe angled along the bushes.

"Where are you going, Joe? It's just about dinnertime, and my motto is: *Never* keep your kibble waiting!"

Wishbone barked, but Joe kept walking, looking under the bushes. Finally, Wishbone's curiosity got the better of him and he ran after Joe.

"What are we looking for? I don't see anything else that could—"

Suddenly, Wishbone picked up a strong, familiar scent under one of the bushes.

"Old, damp felt . . . That championship banner must be around here somewhere!" The Jack Russell terrier pawed the leaves and dug into the earth under the bush. But he saw no sign of the banner. "Hmm . . . That's strange."

"That's strange. I was positive I saw something over here," Joe said. "Maybe I just imagined it."

"No way! This nose *knows* the championship banner was here." Wishbone sniffed around the bush a little longer before giving up. "What I *don't* know is where it is *now.*"

Joe had a hard time focusing on his homework that night. He kept remembering the suspicious looks on his teammates' faces, and it made him feel terrible. It seemed like forever before he was finally done with his assignments and could stretch out on the living room couch with *The Maltese Falcon.*

"At least I know *you* trust me, right, Wishbone?" Joe said, as his pal jumped up onto the couch.

Wishbone barked and wagged his tail, as if to say, "I'm there for you, Joe!"

It's hard to believe, thought Joe, *but right now I feel as if I have more in common with a dog and a fictional character from a book than I do with my own teammates.*

He wouldn't have thought anything in his life could mirror the sneaky things that happened in *The Maltese Falcon.* But there he was, suspected of a crime he didn't commit, just like Sam Spade.

Joe had to hand it to Spade. The detective was as cool as a cucumber. He didn't seem to care if people suspected him of lying, stealing, even killing.

But Joe *did* mind being suspected of stealing and lying. He minded a lot.

"Why would Damont want to turn the other guys against me?" he wondered aloud, as Wishbone curled up at his feet and closed his eyes.

After all, it wasn't that long ago that *Damont* had been falsely accused of stealing a basketball trophy. Joe had given Damont the benefit of the doubt then. Apparently, Damont wasn't willing to do the same for him.

"Does Damont really *believe* I'm the prankster, or is he just setting me up so no one will suspect that it's really *him?*" Joe sighed, staring at the book in his lap. "Or maybe I'm just overreacting because everyone in *here* tries to set up everyone else."

As Joe tapped the cover of *The Maltese Falcon,*

Wishbone opened one eye and barked again. He seemed just as interested in the mystery as Joe was.

Joe was right in the thick of the book now. Brigid O'Shaughnessy and the other characters were always double-crossing one another, selling one another out in order to get their hands on the priceless falcon. Brigid, the very person Sam Spade was supposed to protect, lied to him constantly. Spade still didn't know where the falcon was, and there wasn't anyone he could really trust to help him find it.

Joe felt the same way about the guys on his basketball team. He couldn't count on them to help him find out who the prankster was, because they all thought *he* was responsible for the weird events that had occurred.

"I just hope I can be as good a detective as Sam Spade," Joe said. He smiled as Wishbone's tail thumped against his leg. "At least *you* have faith in me, boy."

Joe knew that his mom, Sam, and David were there for him, too. He'd told them this evening all about what had happened at practice and after practice. But they hadn't been able to answer the questions that kept running through Joe's mind: Who was the prankster? If it was someone on the team, why was he targeting his own teammates? And why would he take an old championship banner?

Whoever it was didn't want to be caught—badly enough to let everyone else believe Joe was the prankster. And badly enough to set a trap to trip up Joe in the woods behind the school.

Joe thought back over the chase and what had happened afterward. He'd spotted that mound among the bushes, and then it was gone. *"Was* it the championship banner?" he wondered aloud.

Wishbone lifted his head, suddenly alert. He barked twice, as if he were trying to tell Joe something.

"Calm down, boy. You're just as frustrated by all these questions as I am, aren't you?"

Joe just hoped they would start finding some *answers* soon.

Wishbone was in his yard Friday afternoon when the mail carrier pulled his cart up out front.

"Hi, Dan!" The terrier wagged his tail and trotted out to the sidewalk. "I don't suppose there are any treats mixed in with all that paper."

"Hello, Wishbone," Dan Bloodgood said as he stepped away from the cart. "I just saw some of your doggie pals over at Jackson Park. Why aren't you with them?"

"Oh, you know how it is." Wishbone sniffed the handful of magazines and envelopes in Dan's hand. "Sometimes a dog's got to do what a dog's got to do— take naps, secure the premises from feline intruders, help Joe find out who's behind some sneaky stuff at basketball practice. . . ."

"I would almost guess you're waiting for something," Dan said, with a knowing nod. "Or some*one.* Say, what about that pretty little Yorkshire terrier I've seen around lately?"

Just hearing Yorkie's name made Wishbone bark

for joy. "You know, for a human, you're very sharp, Dan. I guess I *am* waiting for my pal, Yorkie!"

"I don't know, Wishbone." Dan shook his head slowly. "That terrier may be cute, but I can't say she strikes me as a dog you can count on. She dropped you like a hot potato when Wanda caught you in her garden."

"She didn't mean to." Wishbone looked up earnestly at Dan. "Yesterday she stuck right by me when we raced to get away from Officer Garcia. We played together all afternoon—until the itching-powder emergency behind the school, that is. And that wasn't Yorkie's fault. Trust me, Yorkie and I were meant for each other. We like the same leaf piles, the same dirt, the same bones . . ."

Dan reached down to scratch Wishbone's nose.

Wishbone broke off his conversation when he saw Yorkie emerge from the bushes across from

Wanda's house. She ran right over to Wanda's flower beds, then barked at Wishbone.

"Speaking of that pretty little terrier," Dan said. He raised a warning eyebrow at Wishbone. "Remember what happened last time you went digging over there."

"Sure, but . . ." Wishbone took one look into Yorkie's glistening eyes and ran to join her among the flowers. "I can't resist!"

Yorkie jumped, eagerly pawing at the dirt. She seemed to know that digging up bones was exactly what he was in the mood for.

"Let's play, Yorkie. Wanda won't mind if we dig just a *little*. . . ."

Chapter Eight

Joe was standing at his locker Friday afternoon when he heard David's voice behind him.

"Shouldn't you be at basketball practice, Joe?"

Turning around, Joe saw David walking down the hall toward him. He looked surprised. After all, Joe was *never* late for practice.

"I should be," Joe said. "But it's hard to get psyched about playing when the other guys on the team think I'm trying to hurt them."

Joe had called David and Sam the night before to tell them about the itching-powder incident. It was comforting to talk to friends who believed in him. But that wasn't going to help him on the court.

"*You* know you didn't do anything," David pointed out. "If you don't show up, that just makes you look more guilty. Besides, you can't let Coach Allen down."

"I know, I know." Joe grabbed his sports bag and swung his locker door shut. "Wish me luck. I'm going to need it."

"Good luck," said David. He gave Joe the thumbs-up

sign, but Joe still dragged his feet. By the time he made it to the locker room and changed, the rest of the team was already on the court doing drills.

"Let's hustle, Joe. You're late," Coach Allen called out to him.

Rather than put his towel and water bottle in the corner next to the bleachers, where he usually did, Joe dropped them in a heap at the sidelines. The players were in two lines, taking turns dribbling up and down the court. As Joe joined the end of one line, a few of his teammates glanced over at him. Drew was right in front of him. When he saw Joe, he edged away the slightest bit.

Usually there was a lot of joking around, even though the team members worked hard. Today, Drew didn't even crack a smile when he passed the ball to Joe so he could take his turn. As he started to dribble down the court, Joe tried not to let his teammates' attitude bother him.

But it wasn't easy. . . .

"Not again, Wishbone!"

Wishbone stopped digging when he heard Wanda's shriek coming from somewhere close by. Looking up, he saw her angular face framed by the window overlooking the flower beds. "Uh-oh. Looks like the gardening police are on our tail, Yorkie."

Yorkie kept digging. Tail wagging, she dug deeper into the hole she and Wishbone were working on.

"Now you're leading the neighborhood dogs here

to help you?" Wanda opened the window and called out in a distinctly *un*happy voice. "Wishbone, when are you going to learn to leave my flowers alone?"

"Let's talk about this, Wanda. Maybe you should reconsider where you plant your flowers." Wishbone looked up at Wanda with his biggest smile, but she just scowled.

"Oooooh!" she said angrily. "Wait till I get my hands on you. . . ."

"That's our cue, Yorkie." Wishbone barked, backing away from the flower bed. "We'd better get out of here—fast!"

Yorkie was right on Wishbone's heels. They ran quickly down the street and out of sight of Wanda's house, barking as they went. Wishbone didn't stop running until he and Yorkie reached Jackson Park.

"School's out already?" Wishbone cocked his head to one side, watching a few girls ride past on their bikes. "That means basketball practice has started. Want to come with me, Yorkie? You see, my boy Joe is having trouble. His teammates think he's been pulling some mean tricks, and it's up to *me* to help him find the real prankster."

Wishbone wagged his tail invitingly, but Yorkie just stood there, gazing at him with her big eyes.

"I'd like to stay here and play, but I really have to go to Joe's school. He needs my support." Wishbone took a few steps, then turned back to face Yorkie. "Coming?"

Wishbone didn't see how she could refuse. After all, they were close pals. At least Wishbone thought they were. But Yorkie wasn't even looking at him anymore.

She turned her head first one way, then another, scanning the park. Seeing another dog over by the large oak tree she had visited with Wishbone, she trotted off in that direction. Wishbone sighed as he watched her go.

" 'Bye, Yorkie. See you later . . . I hope."

Wishbone didn't want to leave the park without her, but he couldn't let down his best buddy. Joe needed him!

Wishbone hurried to the school. When a group of girls came out the front door, the terrier snuck inside and went straight to the gym.

As soon as he pushed through the double doors, Wishbone saw that basketball practice was going strong. The boys were in two lines, dribbling and passing the ball down the court, then going for a jump-shot at the basket. The smell of sweat, the sounds of pounding feet, and the fast-moving players were the same as usual. Wishbone's tail wagged as he took in the entire scene.

From what he could see, everything at practice was going fine. There were no more pranks or funny business—at least none he could detect. But something was different. The boys looked so serious—almost nervous. . . .

"Leave the detective work to me, boys, and concentrate on your playing."

Wishbone trotted over to the sidelines as Joe dribbled the ball down the court. He passed to the player from the other line, but the boy stumbled before he could pass back. His sneaker skidded, and the ball went wild.

"Nice save!" Wishbone's tail wagged as Joe leaped

to the left and managed to get a hand on the ball. Joe bounced the ball once, twice, then jumped for the basket. "Yes! Great shot, buddy. You're looking good!"

"That's the second time you've slipped today, Drew," Coach Allen called out. "And you're not the only one. On your toes, boys! Joe, nice shot."

Wishbone barked with pride. But his smile faltered when he saw the hooded glances the boys on the team shot at Joe.

"You can't look at my pal like that. He didn't do anything! But *someone* did. . . ." Wishbone looked curiously from one boy to another. "By the way, is anyone here missing a white sports cap? Because, if you are, I'd like to have a word with you. . . ."

Wishbone saw that Damont was at the front of one line now. As Joe passed the ball to him, Damont gave him a challenging look. "You think you're hot, Talbot?" Damont said under his breath. "If you want to see some smoking moves, check *this* out. . . ."

Damont headed down the court, dribbling the ball in a fancy move under his left leg. He was about to do the same move with his right leg, but he slipped. Damont's feet flew out from under him and he landed flat on his back.

"Ha!" Wishbone was glad Damont wasn't hurt. But after the way he'd been treating Joe lately, it *was* satisfying to see his hot move fizzle out.

"Focus, Damont. Stick with the program," the coach said, frowning. "We're not going to win against Jefferson with moves like that."

Wishbone trotted over to the bleachers, where Marcus, Jimmy, and the other younger boys were sitting. "Hi, guys. I'd like to play, but I'm going to be busy trying to find out who—"

Wishbone sniffed the bag Marcus held.

"Popcorn! How about a few kernels for the dog?"

"Hey, Wishbone." Marcus held out a handful of popcorn, then turned to Jimmy and said, "Damont is the fourth player to slip since we got here. What's going on?"

Wishbone wondered about that, too, but he was even more curious about the popcorn that lay scattered beneath the bleachers. He hurried below, licking up the popcorn. Just as he snapped up the last kernel, the coach called out, "Let's take five, boys. Try to pull yourselves together before team play, okay?"

Joe grabbed his towel and headed across the court to the bleachers.

"Joe!" Wishbone trotted out from under the

bleachers. "Sorry I missed the beginning of practice, but Yorkie and I were—"

Wishbone's paws hit something squishy on the floor, and he slipped.

"Hey! What . . . ?"

Suddenly, he was sliding across the floor on his stomach. He didn't stop until his front paws skidded into Joe's feet.

"Thanks for stopping me, Joe." Wishbone tried to get up, but his paws kept slipping out from under him.

"What's the matter, boy?" Joe asked. He bent down and felt the floor next to Wishbone, then frowned. *"Soap.* There's a whole slick of it here," he said, scanning the area. "No *wonder* everyone was slipping. Hey, Coach, take a look over here!"

Coach Allen stepped over to Joe, with Damont and some other players coming up behind him.

"Allow me to show you Exhibit A. Someone rubbed *this* . . ."—Wishbone said as he rolled over to show everyone the soapy fur on his stomach—". . . on the floor, knowing you guys would step in it!"

"Someone put the soap here on purpose," Damont said. "He *knew* we would step in it."

Wishbone glanced up at Damont and sighed. "Why doesn't anyone ever listen to me?"

"These pranks have gone far enough," Coach Allen said, shaking his head slowly. "If any of you boys know about this, you'd better speak up now."

Damont said nothing, but crossed his arms over his chest and stared straight at Joe.

"Why are you looking at *me?*" Joe asked, frowning.

"I think you know why," Damont said.

"You think *I* put that soap there?" Joe shook his head firmly. "No way."

"Joe is above suspicion, I tell you!" Wishbone barked, scrambling back upright onto all fours. "And just as soon as I stop slipping around, I'll try to sniff out the person who *really* put that soap there."

"First of all, I didn't come anywhere near here until right now," Joe said. "Second of all, the soap is right where I always put my stuff. If I'd gotten to practice on time, *I* would have stepped in it, too. Besides, if I'm the prankster, then why did someone try to trip me up in the woods yesterday?" Joe crossed his arms over his chest and stared back at Damont. "You wouldn't happen to know anything about *that*, would you, Damont?"

Wishbone was proud of the way Joe stood up for himself. "You tell 'em, Joe!"

"Are you telling me there's been *another* prank?" Coach Allen asked, looking at Joe in surprise.

Damont rolled his eyes. "Maybe in Talbot's dreams," he scoffed. "We all know he's not the victim here."

Wishbone gave an angry bark. Damont was as tricky as any cat. Joe had been in danger, and Damont *still* had convinced the other boys to go against him.

"No one's accusing you, Joe," said Coach Allen. He shot Damont a warning look. "Not without something *much* more solid than I've seen so far."

"Yes! We have one supporter. Now, how about the rest of you?" Wishbone trotted over to the other boys and looked up at them. "You're all reasonable guys."

Joe's teammates stood in a line and scowled down

at the soapy area. Wishbone sighed when he saw the suspicious glances they shot toward Joe. Wishbone was just one dog against an army of distrust, but he couldn't give up. "Won't you give Joe a chance, boys? Please?"

Chapter Nine

"Boy, am I glad it's Saturday," said Joe. He, Sam, and David were coasting down the street on their in-line skates. Wishbone ran alongside them, his eyes bright and his tail wagging. "Two whole days of no practice, no pranks, no guys treating me like I'm a criminal. It sure feels good to be with friends." Hearing a bark from Wishbone, he grinned.

"It's kind of a shame," Sam said. She brushed a flyaway strand of blond hair from her face, then coasted ahead. "You love basketball. Damont is so unfair, trying to convince the other guys on the team you're the one who pulled those pranks."

"Being fair has never been very high on Damont's list of priorities," said David.

"That's for sure." Every time Joe thought about his situation, he got angry. "The trouble is, I still don't know who *did* pull the pranks. I thought it might be Damont. It would make sense that he would blame me just so the other guys wouldn't think *he* did anything. But that theory flew out the window after Damont found itching powder in his sneakers."

"Didn't you say he slipped in that soapy spot yesterday, too?" asked Sam. "I just can't picture Damont sabotaging *himself.*"

"Neither can I. That's the problem," said Joe. "If Damont didn't do that stuff, then who *did?*"

Sam and David both looked puzzled as they skated around the corner toward Jackson Park. "A kid from another team?" David suggested. "We're playing Jefferson next week. Maybe one of their guys wants to make *sure* they win by sabotaging our team. They could even have tried to sabotage *you* with that trip cord in the woods."

Joe had already thought about that, but the theory didn't make much sense to him. "Whoever's pulling the pranks has already sneaked into our gym three times," he said. "Once to hide the sports equipment and take the championship flag; once to plant the itching powder; and once to rub soap on the floor. Anyone who isn't from Oakdale would definitely stand out."

"So it's probably someone from our own school . . . maybe even from the basketball team," Sam said. She looked back and forth between Joe and David, frowning. "But who?"

That is the million-dollar question, thought Joe.

With a sigh, he jumped the curb and skated onto one of the walkways that wound inside the park. Wishbone was right behind him, his tail wagging and his tongue lolling. "Come on, Wishbone, let's race!"

Joe skated as fast as he could, with Wishbone

barking at his heels. The crisp breeze felt great against his cheeks. Trees, lampposts, and joggers whizzed by in a blur. With his best buddy by his side, it was easy for Joe to push all thoughts of Damont and the pranks from his head—until the basketball courts came into sight.

Joe stopped about fifty yards away, skating in a slow circle until Sam and David caught up with him.

"It's just my luck that Damont is here," Joe said. He glanced over at the courts, where Damont, Drew, Hank, and a few other guys were playing. "Hank usually calls *me* to shoot hoops on the weekend."

"You can't let them upset you, Joe," Sam said. "You have just as much of a right to be here as they do."

David nodded his agreement. "Besides, avoiding them—"

"I know, I know," Joe interrupted. "It just makes me seem guilty. Well, at least you guys are with me. How bad could it be?"

Joe, Sam, and David coasted the last fifty yards to the basketball courts, with Wishbone running ahead of them. Joe wasn't surprised to see Jimmy Kidd filling Damont's water bottle at the fountain. That kid went *everywhere* Damont did.

"Hi, guys," Joe said, stopping at the edge of the court. "What's up?"

Hank jumped for the layup, then clapped when Damont grabbed the ball on the rebound and made the shot. Joe was sure the guys had seen him, but Hank and Drew barely nodded at him. The other guys ignored him completely.

"See what it's like?" Joe whispered to Sam and David. "I might as well be invisible."

"Excuse me." Jimmy gave Joe a funny look as he hustled past with Damont's water bottle. He placed it on the ground at courtside and called out, "I got fresh water for you, Damont!"

"Can't you see we're busy?" Damont said to Jimmy. When his eyes fell on Joe, the corners of his mouth lifted in a smirk. "What are *you* doing here, Talbot? Haven't you caused enough trouble already?"

"I have just as much right to be here, Damont," Joe replied.

Sam called out to Damont, "This was public property last time I checked."

Shooting Joe a determined look, Sam skated onto the next basketball court, which was empty. Joe hesitated, but only for a second. He wasn't about to give Damont the satisfaction of knowing how much it hurt to be ignored. Joe thought of Sam Spade. Even when the cops and everyone else seemed to be against him, the detective did whatever he had to do to discover the truth about the murders and the Maltese falcon. Joe decided he would stick to his guns, too.

While Wishbone lapped up water from a puddle by a water fountain, Joe and David followed Sam onto the empty court. They skated in wide, fast circles. Joe could feel the stares Damont and the other guys shot at him. Despite his determination, he was starting to get really sick of those looks.

After a few minutes, he said, "I don't need to hang around while these guys judge me."

"It *is* pretty unfair," David agreed. "Anyway, I'm getting hungry. Let's go get some pizza."

"Pizza?" Wishbone jumped up and flipped for joy. His mouth was watering already. "Sounds like a great plan to me. Let's go!"

The terrier trotted happily along on the path next to Joe, Sam, and David. "Saturdays are the best! There's extra play time with Joe, pit stops at Pepper Pete's, *more* pit stops at Pepper Pete's . . ."

Wishbone saw the serious look on Joe's face, and he barked up at him.

"Don't let those boys get you down, Joe. One bite of pepperoni—and I guarantee you'll feel better."

At least, he hoped so. Joe certainly had put up with a lot of abuse on the basketball team lately. Wishbone just hoped they would find the real prankster soon, so Joe would stop frowning so much and life could go back to normal.

Wishbone's tail started to wag furiously when they approached Pepper Pete's a short while later. *Mmm, I can practically taste the pepperoni. . . .*

Wishbone paused when he saw something move at the end of the alleyway next to the pizza parlor. He looked ahead, then barked for joy. "Yorkie? Is that you?"

It had been only a day since he saw her last. Yorkie's white fur looked matted and had lost some of its shine. Still, her inviting brown eyes were as irresistible as ever. Seeing Wishbone, she trotted over to him. She scratched at the entrance to Pepper Pete's, then gazed at him with hungry eyes.

"Wishbone, who's your friend?" said Joe.

"You look starved, Yorkie. Hey, Joe! Can't you find Yorkie's people and tell them to beef up on the kibble?" Wishbone barked, then cocked his head to one side and looked curiously at Yorkie. "You do *have* people, don't you?"

When she didn't answer, Wishbone sighed.

"You sure are a mystery, Yorkie. Kind of like Brigid O'Shaughnessy in *The Maltese Falcon* . . . except much nicer, of course. But no matter. Let's get something to eat!"

"Come on, Wishbone," Joe said. As he opened the door to Pepper Pete's, he turned to Sam and David. "What kind of pizza should we get?"

"Pepperoni!" Wishbone barked out.

"Dad told me the special today is mushroom-and-meatball with extra cheese," Sam said.

"Sounds great," David said. He looked at Joe, who nodded.

They sat down at a table and placed their order.

Wishbone sighed. "Looks like I've been outvoted. But, hey, meatball is fine by me."

Sam's father, Walter Kepler, was the new owner of Pepper Pete's. Wishbone had tasted enough of his pizzas to know that *every* topping was great.

"We've got important work to do, Yorkie. We can't expect to cheer up Joe and find the prankster on an empty stomach, can we?"

Wishbone and Yorkie stood by the doorway, inside the pizza parlor. The smells of cheese, meatballs, pepperoni, and tomato sauce made Wishbone's tongue hang from his mouth.

Wishbone trotted over to the closest table and looked up at a boy who was eating a cheesy slice of pizza.

"Excuse me, but my friend and I are here to make sure the quality of that pizza meets the highest canine standards. . . ."

Wishbone looked up to see Sam's father emerge from the kitchen.

"Hi, Mr. Kepler!"

Sam's father frowned down at Yorkie. "Who let this stray in here?" he asked. Bending down, he scooped up Yorkie. "Sorry, but you've got to go."

"But Yorkie's my friend!" Wishbone barked in alarm. "You can't do that!"

"Can't she stay, Dad?" Sam asked. "She's so cute. And she looks hungry."

Mr. Kepler shook his head. "She's also dirty. I can't let strange mutts in here."

"I object! Yorkie is *not* a mutt." Wishbone followed at Mr. Kepler's heels, but it didn't stop him from putting Yorkie outside. Wishbone watched helplessly as Mr. Kepler gently placed the terrier on the sidewalk outside. What was Wishbone going to do now?

"Stay there, Yorkie!" Wishbone barked as an idea came to him. "I've got a plan."

Wishbone always took his quality-control work very seriously. But knowing that Yorkie was hungry made him put extra energy into it. As he went from table to table, many of the customers recognized him and gave him tidbits.

Fantastic! Wishbone licked his chops after swallowing half a dozen tasty morsels. *Now all I have to do is get some for Yorkie. . . .*

Sniffing the air, he caught the powerful scents of meatballs and cheese. A fresh, mouth-watering pizza sat on a serving tray just behind him. Mmm-mmm! Wishbone knew Yorkie would love it. Of course, the pizza hadn't yet been delivered to a table, but . . .

Before Wishbone could stop himself, he jumped up and his teeth closed around a slice of pizza. The yummy tastes of cheese and meatballs filled his mouth. Wishbone dropped back to the floor with the huge slice hanging from his mouth.

"Wishbone!" Joe, David, and Sam all cried at once.

"That's our pizza!" David added.

Uh-oh. I'm in trouble, thought Wishbone. *But Yorkie needs my help.* He ran to the door as quickly as he could. If he could only get out soon . . .

Just as he reached the door, it swung open. Damont and Jimmy came into Pepper Pete's, and Wishbone scampered out.

"Ffanks, guys," he mumbled through a mouthful of cheese and meatballs. Now . . . where was Yorkie?

Wishbone looked up the street. No Yorkie. He looked down the street—and caught sight of her tail disappearing down the alleyway.

"There you are! Don't go away, Yorkie. I've got something special for you."

Wishbone carried the pizza to the alleyway. When he got there, Yorkie was nothing more than a dark silhouette ten feet away. Wishbone spotted another dog lurking in the shadows, too. They were dragging something along the ground. Wishbone couldn't quite see what it was, but it looked vaguely like an old towel. As he stared at it, Wishbone couldn't help but think there was something familiar about it. . . .

"Yorkie, don't you want some pizza?" Wishbone shook his head back and forth to show her the cheesy slice. She didn't even turn around. "I went to a lot of trouble to get this for you. Aren't you even going to say thanks?"

Apparently not. Yorkie and the other dog kept moving down the alley away from Wishbone. He wondered what could possibly be more interesting than pizza. But when he took another look at the dark, thick fabric, he still couldn't tell what it was.

Wishbone gulped down the pizza, but doing so didn't make him feel much better. His paws were heavy on the sidewalk as he started back to the restaurant to wait for someone to let him back in. How could Yorkie just leave him there? Now he was outside of Pepper Pete's, when he should be inside helping Joe!

"What's this?" Wishbone stopped as his paw landed on something thick and soft. He sniffed, growing excited as he picked up a familiar scent. "I'd know that damp felt aroma anywhere!"

Wishbone grabbed the bit of fabric with his teeth.

"Yup, it's blue felt, all right. No *wonder* the thing Yorkie was dragging along looked familiar. It wasn't a towel. It was the championship banner. This piece must have been torn from it!"

He raced to the door, holding the scrap of felt in his mouth.

"I've got to show this to Joe—pronto!"

Chapter Ten

"What got into Wishbone?" Sam asked, as she reached for her second slice of pizza. "It's not like him to take a whole slice."

"You must not be feeding him enough," David teased, grinning at Joe.

"Yeah, right," Joe said, rolling his eyes. They all knew Wishbone got more than his share of food. But he *had* been acting strange since they had arrived at Pepper Pete's. "Well, taking food *is* a dog thing. And at least it was *our* pizza he ate, not a stranger's."

Joe started to laugh, but it caught in his throat when he saw Damont and Jimmy sitting at a booth across the room.

"When did *they* get here?" he asked. "Can't I even get something to eat without being hounded by Damont?"

Before Sam or David could answer, the door to Pepper Pete's opened. Wishbone ran in ahead of Marcus and Melina Finch, who were with their uncle, Travis Del Rio. Wishbone held something in his mouth, but Joe didn't notice what it was. He was too busy staring at Marcus's head.

"Where's his cap?" Joe murmured, thinking out loud.

"Does he need one?" Sam shot Joe a questioning glance. "It's not like my dad enforces a dress code here."

Joe was so lost in thought that he didn't even laugh at the joke. "His Oakdale Sports and Games cap," he said. "Marcus *always* wears it. But he doesn't have it on now."

"You mean, like the one you found in the woods?" Sam asked. Joe could practically see the light blink on inside her head as she turned to look at Marcus. "You think *he* tried to trip you?"

"It's hard to imagine," Joe admitted. "Marcus is a really nice kid."

"The cap you found in the woods didn't necessarily come from him," David pointed out. "You said yourself that Travis has given out dozens of them."

Joe nodded, keeping his eyes on the boy. "Marcus probably didn't do anything," he said. "Still . . ." Joe stood up suddenly, making up his mind. "I'm going to talk to him. Maybe he saw something, or knows something that might be an important clue. I'll be right back."

Travis Del Rio looked up with a smile when Joe reached their table. "How's it going, Joe? Marcus tells me there's been some trouble on the basketball team the past few days."

Travis always kept an open mind—something Joe really appreciated just then. "Actually, that's why I came over here," Joe said. There was an empty chair at the table, so he sat down and briefly told Travis about the pranks. "I thought Marcus might be able to help me figure out who's responsible for what happened."

"Me?" A confused expression came over Marcus's face. "What can *I* do?"

"Well," Joe began, "I found an Oakdale Sports and Games cap on Thursday, and—"

"Cool!" Marcus exclaimed, his face lighting up. "I hope it's mine. I lost it Thursday, and I've been looking *everywhere* for it. Where did you find it?"

Wishbone pawed at Joe's feet, but Joe kept talking to Marcus. "I found it in the woods," he said, "not far from where Wishbone dug up a tin of itching powder."

Joe patted Wishbone, and the dog tried to put something in his hand.

"Hold on, Wishbone. I'm busy, boy."

Travis looked seriously at Joe. "You don't think *Marcus* is involved, do you?"

"No," Joe said, and he meant it. If Marcus *had* set up that trip cord in the woods, he wouldn't have admitted the cap was his. "But maybe whoever was wearing Marcus's cap had something to do with the pranks," Joe suggested. "Do you know *where* you lost it?"

Marcus shook his head. "All I know is that it was gone when I got home. I was pretty upset about it. I mean, I know I can get another one, but that one was worn in just right."

Joe held back a sigh of disappointment. So much for Marcus leading him to the prankster. "Have you seen anything unusual at basketball practice?" he asked. "Anyone lurking around who isn't usually at practice? Or any of the guys going into the locker room when the rest of us were on the court?"

Marcus shook his head again. "Sorry."

"Maybe even someone who might have been carrying a bar of soap around in the gym?" Travis put in.

"Exactly," said Joe. "Anything at all that seemed out of the ordinary or—"

He broke off as Wishbone dropped something slimy in his lap.

"Yecch!" he said automatically. "Wishbone, I really don't need this smelly piece of— Hey! Is this what I think it is?"

"Looks like trash to me," Travis said, with a laugh.

Taking the bit of blue felt between his thumb and forefinger, Joe held it up for a closer look. "It's from the

championship banner!" he said, spotting part of the banner's gold lettering.

"The one that's missing?" Marcus asked, leaning forward for a closer look. "How did it get *here?*"

"Good question." Joe reached down to scratch Wishbone behind the ears. "Where did you pick this up, boy?"

"As if he could answer, Joe," Melina said with a grin. "Everyone knows dogs can't talk."

"I beg to differ!" Wishbone gave an indignant bark. "You people just don't know how to listen! For your information, *this* . . ."—the terrier nudged the scrap of felt with his muzzle—". . . came from right outside. My pal Yorkie has the rest of it. Come on! I'll show you."

Wishbone barked and trotted toward the door, but no one followed.

"Joe?"

Joe was still staring intently at the blue felt. Finally he let it drop to the table and said, "Oh, well . . . It looks like we may never find out what happened to that banner."

Wishbone sighed. Even Joe wasn't getting the message. What was a dog supposed to do?

"One pepperoni pizza, hot out of the oven!" Walter Kepler announced.

Wishbone perked up as Sam's father placed the pizza in the middle of the table and Travis began passing out slices.

Wishbone gave Marcus his most winning dog smile. "Mr. Kepler may not have mentioned my important quality-control work. You really shouldn't eat that until I've made sure it meets the highest canine standards. . . ."

This time, Marcus seemed to understand him perfectly. Wishbone's tail wagged wildly as Marcus tore a bit from the slice and gave it to him. "Here you go, Wishbone."

"Yes!" Wishbone swallowed it in one bite, then opened his mouth for a bit of crust Melina handed him. "Mmm! Maybe you'd better give me another piece, just to make absolutely sure it's first-rate."

Marcus plucked a circle of pepperoni from his slice and started to hand it to Wishbone. Just as Wishbone's teeth were about to close around it, a voice called to Marcus.

"Hey, Marcus! Why are you talking to Joe?"

Marcus sat straight up, pulling the pepperoni just out of Wishbone's reach. Wishbone's teeth clamped down on thin air. Looking up, he saw that Jimmy Kidd had spoken from a few tables over, where he was eating pizza with Damont.

Jimmy flicked a thumb at Joe and said, "Everyone knows *he* did all that stuff to the basketball team."

Wishbone barked in Joe's defense, but he saw Joe didn't need him. Joe simply said, "That's what you'd like people to think, anyway." With a pointed glance at Damont, he added, "But maybe you're covering up for someone else. . . ."

"N-no way," Jimmy said. But Wishbone didn't miss the uncomfortable glance Jimmy shot at his cousin. Damont just rolled his eyes, but Wishbone didn't trust him any more than he trusted the neighborhood cats. Something was *definitely* fishy about those two.

Joe must have noticed the same thing. "Have either of you seen Marcus's cap around?" he asked Jimmy and Damont, watching them carefully. "It's been missing since Thursday."

"Thanks for the news flash, Talbot. Is there some reason I should care?" Damont scoffed.

"Only if you're the person who set up the cord to trip me out behind the school," Joe shot back.

Damont was as cool and sly as any feline, Wishbone noticed. Jimmy seemed more uneasy. But he followed Damont's lead and rolled his eyes.

"How should *we* know where it is?" Jimmy asked. "Maybe aliens took your cap, Marcus. You know, the kind with three eyes, and feet growing out of their stomachs. . . ."

Within seconds, Jimmy launched into a wild tale about an alien kidnapping. Looking around, Wishbone saw that Marcus was listening closely. He seemed to have totally forgotten about the missing cap and the pranks.

"Hmmm . . ." Wishbone glanced longingly at the pizza on the table. "I like a good story as much as anyone, guys. But all this talking is keeping Marcus from more important matters . . . such as feeding me!"

Chapter Eleven

That evening, Joe leaned against the pillows on his bed. One hand rested on Wishbone's flank, rising and falling with the terrier's breathing. Joe's other hand held his dad's copy of *The Maltese Falcon* propped open on his lap.

Joe had never been so caught up in a mystery before. In the story, Brigid O'Shaughnessy had finally admitted to Sam Spade that she knew where the Maltese falcon was, and that she would be able to get it soon. Spade learned that she had double-crossed some other people in order to get the falcon. Now those people would do anything—even kill Brigid—in order to snatch the statue from her.

To complicate matters even more, Brigid had suddenly disappeared. For the last hour Joe had been reading, spellbound, as Sam Spade followed a winding trail of clues, trying to find both Brigid and the Maltese falcon. Joe had just gotten to the part where the police were questioning Spade yet again about the murders of his partner and Floyd Thursby.

"Why can't those guys leave Sam Spade alone?" Joe muttered aloud. He scratched behind Wishbone's ears, and the dog's tail thumped.

The police in the story didn't even know about the Maltese falcon. They kept grilling Sam Spade, but all their questions just prevented Spade from doing his job—locating Brigid and the falcon.

"It's a lot like what's been happening to me, huh, Wishbone?" Joe said.

At the sound of his name, Wishbone cocked his head to one side and gazed up at Joe.

"The cops keep getting in Spade's way. And the other guys on my team keep fouling things up for *me*. They're so busy suspecting me of being the prankster, it's hard for me to be a part of the team."

Wishbone licked Joe's hand gently, his tail still thumping rhythmically. It was as if he were trying to tell Joe he understood what he was going through.

"The guys on the team could learn a thing or two about loyalty and fairness from you, boy," Joe said.

Wishbone let out a bark that sounded like a happy agreement. Seeing the warmth in the terrier's eyes, Joe had to smile.

Maybe it was silly, but having Wishbone nearby made Joe feel a little better about his situation. Who could tell? Maybe tomorrow the real prankster would be caught, and life would return to normal.

Joe certainly hoped so.

"I want everyone back on the court for team play," Coach Allen called out Monday afternoon.

Joe dropped his towel in the corner next to the bleachers. "One more drink," he told Wishbone. He squirted a stream of water at the terrier's mouth, and Wishbone lapped it up. Then Joe left his water bottle with his towel and jogged onto the court.

Wishbone trotted to the sidelines and sat there. Joe could see the dog's alert eyes following his every move. It was as if Wishbone were looking out for him, but Joe still felt nervous. He half-expected something to go wrong. But the team had been practicing for more than an hour, and so far nothing out of the ordinary had happened. Maybe the pranks were over for good.

Not that it's doing me *any good,* thought Joe. During drills, Damont and several other players had cut in front of him, or passed to the player behind Joe when they should have passed to Joe. Coach Allen came down hard on anyone who treated Joe unfairly, but that still didn't stop the guys from acting up. They continued to shut him out, and Joe was getting very annoyed by their unfair actions.

Don't let it get to you, he told himself. *You're here to play basketball, not to go on trial for something you didn't even do.*

"Okay, boys . . ." The coach looked over the huddle of boys, pointing out five players for each team. The A-team consisted of Damont, Drew, and three other boys. Joe, Hank, and three others were chosen to be the B-team. "Okay, let's move!"

The coach blew his whistle, and the two forwards tipped off. Damont got a hand on the ball and tapped it to Drew. Joe moved in quickly to cover him. He pushed everything from his mind except the game—playing his best and working with his team. He kept his eyes on Drew, watching his every move and trying to gauge what he might do next. When Drew tried to pass, Joe was right there. He jumped left and deflected the ball, sending it right to Hank.

"Nice steal, Joe," Coach Allen called out. "I want to see some hustle, A-team!"

Joe felt a rush of adrenaline. He ran downcourt, then stopped when he realized Hank was in trouble. Damont had cornered him, and none of the other B-team players were open. Joe rushed back, and Drew immediately closed in on him. Joe didn't see any way around him—unless he could fake Drew out. . . .

He started to move left. As soon as Drew moved to cover him, Joe twisted quickly to the right and rushed past him. Yes! He'd done it.

"Here!" he called out to Hank.

Joe was wide open, but Hank hesitated to pass to him, a flash of distrust in his eyes. Instead of passing to Joe, he shot a bounce-pass to another player who was heavily guarded. The boy shot out his hands, but the A-team beat him to the ball.

"Good defense, A-team," said the coach. "Hank, next time think about passing to someone who's open!"

"*If* you can trust him," Damont muttered. He glared openly at Joe.

Joe felt as if a dark cloud had surrounded him. He wasn't just playing against the A-team. Even his own teammates on the B-team were playing against him!

Taking a deep breath, he told himself, *Give it another try.* But the next time the B-team got the ball, the same thing happened. The other guys on his team simply would not work with him.

"This is ridiculous," he said under his breath.

Just then, Damont got the ball and started to dribble quickly toward the basket. Hank was supposed to cover him, but Joe was closer. Moving as fast as he could, he lunged for the ball. Damont jumped back, but he was a second too late. Before he could dribble the ball out of reach, Joe grabbed it.

"Nice!" said the coach. "Let's see some teamwork, B-team!"

Joe started to look for a teammate he could pass to, then changed his mind. They wouldn't *let* him be a team player, so why bother? Just like Sam Spade, he was on his own.

Joe heard Wishbone's bark and spotted the dog on the sidelines, his tail wagging. *Well, not* totally *alone. I've got one fan, anyway,* Joe thought.

"You're dead, Talbot." Damont charged toward him, his face flushed and angry.

"Oh, yeah?" Joe shot back. As Damont moved in for the steal, Joe twisted around him and dribbled the ball out of reach.

"Don't forget the rest of your team, Joe!" Coach Allen called, but Joe ignored him. For once, he was going to look out for himself.

He blew past Damont, keeping his eyes on the basket up ahead. Joe was vaguely aware of his team-mates, but he didn't even try to pass to them. He ran downcourt, dribbled around the A-team guard,

then sent the ball flying through the air. It hit the backboard, then dropped through the hoop.

"All right!" he cried.

Let the other guys think whatever they want about me, Joe thought. He wasn't going to let anything get in the way of playing his best. If that meant hot-rodding a little bit, so what?

Joe poured all of his frustrations into the game—moving in relentlessly on the A-team, stealing the ball, making every shot he could instead of worrying about passing. He managed to steal the ball from Damont twice. And at the end of team play, he had scored fifteen of his team's twenty-one points. Joe felt great—until he saw the look on Coach Allen's face.

"What happened to teamwork, Joe?" Coach Allen asked, as Joe and the other boys walked off the court.

Joe couldn't make himself look the coach directly in the eye. *It's not* my *fault teamwork is taking a nosedive,* he wanted to say. But he couldn't bring himself to speak the words out loud. He took a long drink from his water bottle so he wouldn't have to answer.

Wishbone trotted over from the sidelines. He nosed Joe's towel, then gazed up at Joe with eyes that seemed filled with concern. As Wishbone's gaze shifted to the other players, Joe had the feeling his pal was trying to understand what had gone wrong.

I wish I knew, thought Joe.

With a sigh, he grabbed his towel. "Sorry, Coach. Come on, Wishbone," he said.

But as he headed for the locker room, Joe could feel the coach's disappointed gaze boring into his back.

Chapter Twelve

"I know I left my squeaky toy around here some-where. But where?" Wishbone sniffed his way across the living room floor Monday evening, following the faint smell of rubber. When he got to the couch, where Joe and Ellen were sitting, he crouched down and peered between their legs. "Aha!"

Tail wagging, he nosed the bright green rubber toy from beneath the couch and grabbed it with his teeth. Then he looked expectantly at Joe and Ellen.

"Anyone up for some after-kibble games?"

Wishbone gave a happy bark when Joe took the toy from him. But Joe's heart didn't seem to be in it. He barely even looked at Wishbone.

"I can't believe I let Coach Allen down today, Mom," Joe said. He sat back with a sigh, tossing the toy back and forth from one hand to the other. "I *want* to work with the team. But it's difficult when everyone treats me like I'm the enemy."

Wishbone didn't like to see Joe looking so down. "You've still got friends here, buddy. Ellen and I will support you, no matter what!" Jumping onto the couch, Wishbone rested his head on Joe's lap.

"Can't you try reasoning with the other guys?" Ellen suggested.

"Been there. Done that. We tried our best, Ellen, but they wouldn't listen." Wishbone's eyes followed the squeaky toy's progress through the air. "Can I have that back, please, Joe?"

"Damont has totally convinced everyone I pulled those pranks. How can I be a team player when no one trusts me anymore?" said Joe. He scowled, dropping Wishbone's squeaky toy onto the couch. "Every time I'm on the court, it's me against everyone else. Maybe I should just quit."

"What!" Wishbone was so shocked he didn't even pick up his toy. "But you love basketball. You're one of the best players on the team. They need you!"

"It's your decision, Joe," Ellen said slowly. "But if you *do* quit, you'll be giving up on yourself *and* on the team. Do you really think that's the best solution?"

Joe took a deep breath and let it out slowly. "I guess not," he said. "But what else *can* I do?"

Ellen smiled and said, "Sooner or later, the real prankster will be caught. Once that happens, things will go back to normal. You'll see."

"I hope so," said Joe. But he didn't look or sound convinced.

"You've already done a few things to find out who the person is," Ellen pointed out. "You found the itching powder *and* the cap worn by the prankster. You even found a piece of the championship banner."

"I'll take the credit for that, thank you." Wishbone wagged his tail proudly. "Anyway, Ellen is right, Joe. With you and me sniffing out clues, we're bound to track down the bad guy. You have to admit, we make a great team of detectives." Wishbone licked Joe's hand, then grabbed his squeaky toy and dropped it in Joe's lap. "So, are you ready to play now?"

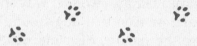

"It's a brand-new day. . . . Yippee!" Wishbone raced out the front door ahead of Ellen on Tuesday morning. The spongy grass felt wonderful under his paws. The air was filled with the smells of dew and leaves.

"Don't get into trouble while I'm at work, Wishbone," Ellen called as she slung her bag over her shoulder and headed for her Explorer.

"Me? No way." Wishbone trotted out toward the sidewalk, glancing all around him. "I'm looking for fun, not trouble. Maybe a romp around the park with my pals before heading over to Joe's school to nose around for clues—"

"Ellen, wait!" Wanda called out.

Wishbone turned to see Wanda rushing across her yard, waving a sheet of paper. Wishbone barked a cheerful hello. "What's the hurry, Wanda? Is there a sale on doggie treats?"

"Good morning, Wanda," Ellen said. "What do you have there?"

"This," said Wanda. She held out the paper to Ellen. "These posters are all over town, about a lost dog. I think it's that Yorkshire terrier I saw in my garden with Wishbone the other day. Do you recognize her?"

"Yorkie?" Wishbone's ears perked up. He rose up on his hind legs to get a look at the photograph on the poster. As soon as he glimpsed the big eyes and gorgeous silky fur, he knew it was her. "Wow! So Yorkie *does* have a family. I wonder why she ran away."

"I think I *have* seen that dog around here," Ellen said, studying the picture. "Let me write down that phone number."

As Ellen searched in her bag for a pen, Wishbone saw something move at the edge of the wooded area across the street. He yelped in surprise when he saw Yorkie appear from under the branches of a thick holly tree.

"Great news, Yorkie! Your people are looking for you." Wishbone barked and trotted across the street.

"Look over there! Isn't that a Yorkshire terrier?" Wanda cried. She squinted at Yorkie. "She's a little dirtier than the dog in the picture, but I think it's her. I'm going to call this number right now. Do me a favor and see if she's got any tags, all right?"

"Take my word for it, she doesn't," Wishbone barked to Ellen as she walked slowly toward him and Yorkie. Then he turned back to Yorkie, his tail wagging back and forth. "Yorkie, did you hear that? With any luck, you'll be back with your own family in time for dinner!"

He expected Yorkie to give a happy bark and romp with him. Instead, she stood frozen, her eyes warily watching Ellen's approach.

"You don't have to worry about Ellen. She's

family. The best." Wishbone tried to reassure Yorkie. "I can't wait to meet *your* family. How about getting your people to invite me over for evening kibble and— Yorkie?"

Yorkie started to bark angrily at Ellen, baring her teeth.

"I won't hurt you," Ellen said in a soothing voice. "I just want to see if you've got tags."

Yorkie backed away from Ellen. Jumping around, she ran back into the woods.

"Yorkie, wait!" Wishbone barked after the white terrier as she disappeared behind the holly branches. Ellen hurried to the holly tree, scanning the woods. "We might never find her now," she murmured. "And I've got to get to work."

"Never fear, Ellen. *I'll* try to talk to her." Wishbone bounded into the woods, squeezing past the thick branches of the holly tree. "You can stop running, Yorkie. It's just me."

The rustling of leaves and tree branches told him Yorkie wasn't too far ahead of him. Wishbone ran past some squirrels and through a stand of oaks before he spotted Yorkie's tail peeking out from behind the trunk of a maple.

"There you are!" Wishbone bounded over to the maple.

Yorkie looked carefully out from behind the maple tree. She seemed to check to make sure he was alone. Only then did she jump playfully in the dead leaves. She rolled on her back, gazing at him with her playful eyes.

Wishbone stopped to sniff the burrs that were matted in Yorkie's fur. "Why didn't you tell me you have a family? Are they nice?"

Yorkie jumped onto all fours and pounced on a nearby stick, growling as she grabbed it. Wishbone sighed. Once again, it looked as if she wasn't giving out any answers.

Taking the other end of the stick in his teeth, Wishbone gave a playful tug. As they dragged it over the leaves, Wishbone remembered something *else* he'd seen Yorkie drag along. He dropped the stick and barked out a question.

"Remember that blue felt thing I saw you with outside Pepper Pete's, Yorkie? Where did you get it?"

Wishbone waited, his tail wagging. Yorkie looked at him for a second, then picked up the stick and trotted away.

"Won't you answer me?" Wishbone waited hopefully, but Yorkie didn't look back.

Wishbone didn't like to admit it, but he was beginning to get the feeling Dan Bloodgood may have been right about Yorkie. The only dog she seemed to care about was herself. For a little dog, she sure could cause a lot of trouble.

"But she's so much fun to play with."

Wishbone gave a big sigh. For all the trouble she'd caused, he still felt a bond with the silky terrier. Somehow, he couldn't imagine simply letting Yorkie go.

With a loud bark, Wishbone trotted through the woods after her. "Wait up! I'm coming, too!"

Chapter Thirteen

Joe sat on the bleachers with his teammates at the start of practice Tuesday afternoon. Coach Allen paced up and down in front of them. He was frowning darkly, and Joe had a feeling he knew why.

"I know we don't usually practice the day before a game," Coach Allen began. "But yesterday's poor performance and lack of teamwork have me worried."

Joe's cheeks burned. He knew he was partly at fault, and he felt badly about it. Looking down, Joe saw Wishbone under the bleachers. The terrier glanced up at Joe and wagged his tail, as if to say, "I have faith in you, buddy!" But it didn't make Joe feel any better.

"I thought you boys wanted to be winners," the coach continued.

"We do," Damont spoke up.

A couple of the guys mumbled their agreement, but the coach merely said, "Well, you haven't been acting like it lately. The Bobcats are tough competition under the best of circumstances. If you boys can't pull together as a *team* . . ."—he emphasized that word, looking sternly from player to player—". . . our winning streak will be over as of tomorrow."

There was complete silence in the gym. Seeing the serious expressions on his teammates' faces, Joe guessed they felt as badly as he did. *No more showing off,* he promised himself. *From now on, I'm going to concentrate on what's best for the Bulldogs.*

"All right, then . . ." Coach Allen clapped his hands, breaking the silence. "Everyone on the court!"

The guys jumped into action. A couple of Joe's teammates actually nodded at him. Joe thought he sensed a new agreement to pull together—until he saw Damont. Damont stood a few feet away with his arms crossed over his chest. The look he shot at Joe was anything but friendly.

So much for camaraderie, Joe thought with a sigh. But, regardless of Damont's attitude, Joe decided to work *with* the other players.

Coach Allen huddled with the starting team, which included Joe, Damont, Drew, and two other players. "Let's work on the combination you were practicing last week," the coach instructed. "Drew, you pass the ball cross-court to Joe. Joe fakes left, then passes right to Damont, who goes for the shot. Got it?"

They all nodded. As Damont tipped off against the forward from the other practice team, Joe felt pumped. Maybe it wasn't too late to pull together.

"All right!" Joe crowed as Damont tipped the ball to Drew. Joe shot forward, feeling a burst of adrenaline. Glancing over his shoulder, he saw Drew maneuver the ball around the defense. *Perfect!* Joe thought. Keeping his eye on the defense, he moved into place for the pass. *I'm open,* he thought. *Pass now!*

From across the court, Drew spotted Joe. He bounced the ball once, then hurled it through the air. *Yes!* thought Joe. There was no way any of the defensive players could beat him to it.

But as Joe reached for the ball, Damont started to move in front of him. "What . . . ?"

Joe couldn't believe it. Damont was trying to steal the ball from him—and they were on the same team!

"No way." Gritting his teeth, Joe twisted around Damont and threw his arms out—just in time. He caught the ball, then quickly dribbled around Damont.

"Hey!" Damont's annoyed cry came from behind Joe, but Joe ignored it.

Concentrate on playing, Joe told himself.

As the defense closed in, Joe faked left, as the coach had instructed. He looked right, but Damont wasn't there for the pass. He had been so busy trying to get the ball from Joe, he wasn't in position. And the other team was closing in fast.

Joe just barely managed to dribble around the defensive guard. He didn't see anyone open, so he jumped for the shot. The ball hit the backboard, but missed the basket. Joe groaned when the other team got the ball on the rebound. He had blown it. Coach Allen blew his whistle to stop play.

"You call that teamwork?" he said, clearly annoyed. "Damont, I don't want to see you pull anything like that again. That goes for you, too, Joe."

"I tried to pass, Coach," Joe began to explain, "But—"

"I don't want to hear it," Coach Allen said abruptly, cutting him off. "Let's try again. And this time I want to see a passing game. There are no superstars on this team, boys."

"Except one," Damont said, keeping his voice low. "And it isn't you, Talbot."

Joe kept his mouth shut, but it wasn't easy.

They tried the combination a few more times. Damont managed to follow the coach's instructions—once. But the second time, Joe caught Damont angling toward him from behind again.

"That pass is mine, Damont," Joe said over his shoulder. "Stick to the game plan."

"Why? So you can find another way to foul up our playing?" Damont said under his breath. "What's it going to be today, Talbot? Greasing the basketball?"

Just then, Drew let the ball go in a long pass across

court to Joe. Damont leaped in front of Joe and grabbed the ball. Joe's face felt red-hot. He was so angry he could hardly see. The moment Damont's hands closed in on the ball, something inside Joe snapped.

Spinning around, Joe lunged toward Damont. Before Damont had taken more than a step, Joe grabbed the ball back. He flew left, dribbling around Damont, then jumped for the shot. The ball arced through the air and *whooshed* through the hoop. It all happened so quickly, Joe hardly knew what he'd done.

Coach Allen blew his whistle. "Practice is over, boys," he said, his voice tired and disappointed. "You all better hope for good luck tomorrow, because we're going to need it."

Joe turned to look at the coach, but instead he found himself face to face with Damont.

"Nobody messes with me like that," Damont said.

Joe's common sense told him just to walk away from Damont, to ignore him. But he had put up with enough abuse. He was going to tell Damont exactly what was on his mind. Joe faced Damont squarely and said, "You've been unfair, Damont, and I've had enough. Can't stand to see someone beat you at your own game?"

"*No one* beats me . . ." Damont shot back, his eyes flashing with anger. "You think you're hot, Talbot? Prove it! One on one, tonight, in Jackson Park."

Joe didn't bat an eye. The other guys had gathered around him and Damont, but he was only vaguely aware of them.

"I'll be there," Joe replied.

Chapter Fourteen

"Finally, the moment I've been waiting for . . ."
Wishbone watched longingly while Joe and Ellen
cleared the table after dinner Tuesday night. "Left-
overs!"

"Here you go, Wishbone," said Ellen. She scraped
some meat into Wishbone's dish, but she seemed
distracted. A few bits missed his dish and tumbled
onto the floor. Wishbone bit into them right away.

"*Mmm-mmm*. Steak . . . my favorite!" He licked
his chops, then glanced up at Ellen's worried face. "Is
everything all right?"

Ellen turned to Joe with a sigh. "Joe, do you really
think it's a good idea for you to play Damont tonight?"
she said.

So *that* was why Ellen was so troubled, Wishbone
realized. She was worried about Joe. Not that Wishbone blamed her. "My sentiments exactly! Listen to
your mother, Joe."

Joe looked up from the sink with a frown. "I *have*
to play him, Mom," he said.

Wishbone sympathized with Joe. His situation was a lot like Sam Spade's in *The Maltese Falcon*. Spade found himself up against some sneaky, mean-spirited characters. The detective was at times searched at gunpoint, punched, and knocked unconscious. But he didn't back off the case. Apparently, Joe wasn't backing down, either.

"I'm proud of you, Joe, but . . . don't you think tonight's challenge will only make the situation more tense than it already is? Shouldn't you think about what's best for the team?" Ellen said.

"I can't let Damont think I'm scared to—"

Wishbone's ears perked up as the doorbell rang. "Someone's here!"

He ran to the front door, barking. When Joe opened the door a moment later, Sam and David were standing there.

"Hi, guys!" Wishbone wagged his tail and gave Sam and David a big smile.

"We have to talk, Joe," David said as he and Sam came inside.

"That's just what Ellen and I were doing." Wishbone followed as Sam, David, and Joe went into the living room. "There are four of us, Joe. Now you *have* to listen."

"We heard about the one-on-one game between you and Damont," Sam said. "You can't play him, Joe. Tomorrow's the big game against the Jefferson Bobcats."

"So?" Joe said, shrugging. Wishbone recognized the stubborn look on his face. He was like a dog who would do anything rather than give up his bone.

"Hi, Sam. Hi, David." Ellen appeared, wiping her hands on a kitchen towel. "Joe and I were just talking about this, as a matter of fact. I'm glad you feel the same way I do."

"And me!" Wishbone let out a bark.

"The team is counting on you and Damont," David told Joe. "If you wear yourselves out tonight, you won't be able to play your best tomorrow."

"We're not playing our best, anyway," Joe pointed out. "And it's mostly because Damont keeps trying to make sure the other guys turn against me. I have to stand up to him, or they'll *never* respect me."

Sam shot David a worried look. "You can't let Damont get to you," she told Joe. "You need to be able to give a hundred percent in tomorrow's game. Otherwise, you'll be letting down the coach, the school, and yourself."

"Not to mention your dog." Wishbone rolled over on the rug, kicking up his paws. "I *am* the official team mascot, after all."

"That's a chance I'll have to take," Joe said firmly. "You can't talk me out of it, guys. I've made up my mind."

Wishbone let out a sigh and rested his chin on Joe's sneakers. "I'm still against it. But if you insist on playing, at least let me come along. Tonight, I'll be *your* official mascot!"

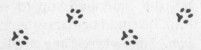

"You guys don't have to come with me," Joe told Sam and David a half-hour later.

Wishbone trotted alongside as they walked toward Jackson Park. "And leave you to face Damont on your own? No way."

"We figure you could use the support," Sam said, smiling at Joe. "Besides, David and I can keep an eye on things while you're playing."

"It can't hurt to get an outsider's perspective," David added. "If Damont *did* pull all those pranks, maybe we'll spot something that proves it."

"Good thinking. I'll put my nose to work, too." Wishbone sniffed the air and looked up at Joe. "I *have* been called the Sam Spade of the canine world, you know."

Joe stared down at the sidewalk, frowning. He bounced his basketball as he walked. "Some detective I am," he mumbled in frustration. "I still haven't figured out who's responsible for the pranks. I keep trying to think like Sam Spade, but so far it's not doing me much good."

"What do you think Sam Spade would do if he were in your shoes?" Sam asked.

"Well," Joe began, "Spade doesn't miss a single detail. . . ."

"Just like yours truly." Wishbone wagged his tail proudly, sniffing the air.

"And he has great instincts when it comes to people," Joe added. "That's where I run into trouble. My *instincts* tell me Damont is up to something. I mean, I still think he could be harassing me so no one will suspect *him*. Plus, every time I talk to Jimmy, he shoots Damont these funny looks—like they have something to hide."

"But we already decided that Damont wouldn't sabotage himself," David put in.

Joe nodded. "And the clues have all led to nothing but dead ends. A tin of itching powder I can't trace to anyone . . . A cap that was taken from Marcus, but I don't know who took it . . ." He continued to tick off the clues one by one on his fingers. "A piece of the championship banner that turned up at Pepper Pete's . . ."

"But we don't know how it got there," Sam finished. "I see what you mean. I bet even Sam Spade would have a tough time with this one."

"You said it." Wishbone barked, wagging his tail.

"Spade seemed to have better luck than I do, anyway," Joe said. "After spending most of the book following clues, in the end he doesn't have to do anything to find the Maltese falcon. It comes right to him."

Sam and David looked at Joe in surprise. "You're kidding," said Sam. "How?"

"That's where the mystery really heats up!" Wishbone said. Thinking about it made Wishbone so excited he kicked up his hind paws. "You see, Brigid O'Shaughnessy arranged for someone else to hide the falcon and—"

"Brigid convinced someone to hide the falcon," said Joe.

"Didn't I just say that?" Wishbone let out a sigh. "Okay, you tell it, Joe."

"But while Brigid was getting the Maltese falcon from him, the other people who were after it tracked them down," Joe went on.

"Uh-oh," said Sam. "Sounds like trouble."

Joe nodded. "I'll say. They shot the guy trying to get the falcon from him."

"Ouch. But then, how did Sam Spade end up with it?" David asked.

"Well . . ." said Joe. He kept his eyes on the basketball as he spoke, dribbling it against the sidewalk. "The man made it to Sam Spade's office with the falcon before he died. Afterward, there's a big confrontation among Brigid, Sam Spade, and all the people who've been chasing after the falcon."

Wishbone never tired of hearing the story of Sam Spade and the Maltese falcon. As he listened to Joe, he kept his ears cocked so he wouldn't miss a word. "Here comes the big surprise. . . ."

"They examine the falcon, and guess what?" Joe stopped dribbling the ball and shook his head in amazement. "It's a fake!"

"What!" David exclaimed. "You mean, they were all trying to kill one another for something that wasn't even worth anything?"

Joe nodded and let out a sigh. "I guess that's one way my life *isn't* like Sam Spade's. I mean, at least I *know* I'm fighting for something worthwhile—my reputation. That's why I have to stand up to Damont."

Wishbone wagged his tail and smiled up at Joe. "Whatever happens, *I* know you're a winner, Joe."

When they reached Jackson Park, Wishbone paused on the sidewalk. He stared at a familiar square truck that was stopped at the edge of the park. "I'd know that Animal Control van anywhere. It's Officer Garcia's."

As Joe, Sam, David, and Wishbone passed the truck, the animal-control officer leaned out her window and asked, "Have any of you seen a stray terrier? White?"

Wishbone didn't like the way Officer Garcia was looking at him. "I am *not* a stray. And neither is Yorkie! She has a family, for your information."

"Is there a problem, ma'am?" Joe asked.

Officer Garcia gave a businesslike nod. "Afraid so," she said. "A woman over on Sharon Circle reported that a terrier attacked her about an hour ago. The dog in question stole some ribs hot off the grill and grabbed a pair of tongs. Knocked the woman over and ripped her dress while escaping the premises. That's a Class-C violation. I'll have to take the dog in."

"It wasn't Wishbone. He was at home with me," Joe reported.

"And it couldn't have been Yorkie. She would never do something like that." Wishbone stood rigidly on the grass and gave an angry bark. "How about doing something truly worthwhile, like rounding up stray *cats.*"

Turning away from Officer Garcia, Wishbone trotted into the park. He was glad when Joe, David, and Sam followed. After all, they had bigger things to worry about than some missing ribs. . . .

Before long, Wishbone saw the basketball courts ahead of them. A group had already gathered beneath one of the baskets. Damont was there, along with several of his Bulldogs teammates. Wishbone wasn't surprised to see Jimmy there, too. He was standing on the sidelines with Marcus and a few other younger boys. Wishbone knew Damont's biggest fan would never miss such an important match.

"This is it, Joe," said Sam, giving him an encouraging smile. "Good luck."

"We'll be rooting for you," added David.

"Especially me!" Wishbone licked Joe's hand, then watched as Joe squared his shoulders and strode onto the blacktop.

As Joe approached Damont, a silence fell over the crowd. For a long while, Joe and Damont just stood there looking at each other.

Wishbone's alert eyes flickered back and forth between the two boys. "Are you guys going to play, or is this staring match going to go on forever?"

"Ready to get toasted, Talbot?" Damont asked, breaking the silence.

"We'll see who's toast when the game's over," Joe shot back.

Wishbone admired Joe's firm stance and steady voice. The terrier glanced expectantly at the faces around the court. "Come on, guys. Can't you see Joe would never do anything to—"

Wishbone broke off suddenly, staring into the trees next to the basketball courts.

"Yorkie! Is that you?" He let out a loud bark of surprise.

The white terrier scampered from the woods with her tail wagging. Dinky was right behind her. The chihuahua dragged something across the grass, but

Wishbone was too busy staring at Yorkie to notice what it was.

"Yorkie, are those tongs in your mouth? *Barbecue* tongs?" Wishbone couldn't believe his eyes. "No. They can't be. . . ."

But they were. When Wishbone trotted over and sniffed the tongs, he saw they were dripping with a thick, sweet-smelling barbecue sauce. There was a smudge of the barbecue sauce on Yorkie's nose, too. And a few rib bones were scattered across the grass nearby. Wishbone licked at the sauce, then stared at a scrap of flowered fabric that clung to the burrs of Yorkie's tail.

"Uh-oh. I think I know where that came from. Yorkie, are *you* the terrier who knocked down that woman and stole those ribs? How could you do such a thing! Dinky, did you talk her into doing it?"

Wishbone turned toward Dinky, but stopped when he caught sight of Officer Garcia. She was making her way across the grass toward them.

"There's the law! She's looking for you, Yorkie—and I don't think it's to hand out dog biscuits." Wishbone barked a warning. "You'd better run for it!"

Yorkie glanced around expectantly. She stiffened when she caught sight of Officer Garcia in her brown uniform. Still holding the tongs, the Yorkshire terrier looked back and forth from Wishbone to Officer Garcia. Then she started to back away from the animal-control officer.

"Don't worry about the bones, Yorkie. I'll save them for you."

Wishbone bent to pick up the closest rib. As his

teeth were about to close around it, he felt Yorkie's warm, ticklish breath right next to him.

In the next moment, he felt something cold and metallic slip over his head. Wishbone felt as if his muzzle were being pinched by a giant pair of tweezers.

"Yuck! Yorkie, get it off!" Wishbone shivered and shook, but he couldn't wriggle free. It took him a moment to realize what was pressing so uncomfortably against his head. "It's the tongs! They're stuck on me. Yuck!"

He backed up, trying to shake the metal things loose. They didn't budge.

"Yorkie, what if Officer Garcia thinks *I* stole these and attacked that woman? Help me get them off!"

Yorkie trotted away from Wishbone without answering.

Just before she disappeared behind a laurel bush, Wishbone had a terrible thought. "Did you do that on *purpose*, Yorkie? Did you set me up?"

"You're a tricky little fellow." Officer Garcia's voice came from right behind Wishbone. "But I've got you now. . . ."

"Me?" Wishbone turned to see the officer walking toward him. "I didn't do anything! Hey, Joe . . . *Help!*"

Wishbone scanned the basketball court, but Joe and Damont were looking for a coin to flip to see who would get the ball first. No one seemed to notice Officer Garcia closing in on Wishbone.

"It wasn't me, I tell you. It was . . ."

Wishbone backed away from the animal-control officer. Glancing back, he spotted Yorkie lurking in the

121

bushes. He didn't want to turn her in, but . . . how could she betray him like that?

As he watched Yorkie dig up some leaves, Wishbone made the toughest decision of his life.

"I thought you were special, Yorkie. But maybe you *are* just like Brigid O'Shaughnessy."

Wishbone recalled that in *The Maltese Falcon,* Sam Spade had found out Brigid was the one who had killed his partner. He had turned Brigid in to the police, even though it broke his heart to do so.

Wishbone backed farther away from Officer Garcia, still trying to shake off the barbecue tongs. *How could I have let Yorkie do this to me!*

"I *won't* let you get away with it, Yorkie!" The Jack Russell terrier ran away from Officer Garcia as quickly as he could, given that the bulky tongs were still clamped tightly to his muzzle. With a determined bark, he headed straight toward the wooded spot where Yorkie stood.

"Officer, I believe the dog you're looking for is right here!"

Chapter Fifteen

Wishbone rounded the laurel bush, with Officer Garcia in hot pursuit. He had led Officer Garcia right to Yorkie. "Looks like I may have found my canine offender," she murmured. Before Yorkie could run, the officer reached down and scooped the terrier into her arms. "A white terrier. And no tags to boot. That's exactly what the victim reported."

Yorkie gazed at Wishbone with wounded eyes. Wishbone could hardly bring himself to look back at her. *She ran out on you. She set you up!* he reminded himself. *Besides, Yorkie's family misses her. They want her back.*

Wishbone knew he had done the right thing. But that didn't make it any easier to see Yorkie go.

The Jack Russell terrier watched the Animal Control van until it disappeared around the corner. His kibble felt heavy in his stomach.

The sounds of paws scratching the dirt made Wishbone turn around. Dinky stood a few feet away. Wishbone had been so busy with Yorkie that he had almost forgotten about the chihuahua. Dinky was still dragging something along the ground. It was torn and covered with dirt and leaves. Wishbone couldn't tell what it was, but it looked and smelled awfully interesting.

"What do you have there, Dinky?" Wishbone was so curious he couldn't help feeling just a little less sad. He trotted over and sniffed—then crouched down and wagged his tail. "Hey! I know that smell! It's the championship banner!"

The dark blue color of the felt was barely recognizable under all that dirt and grit. And the gold letters had turned almost black. But there was no mistaking the damp scent or the texture of the banner. As Dinky shook it in his mouth, Wishbone jumped around him, barking.

"Joe, look what I found! Hey, *Joe!*"

Damont was just about to toss a quarter in the air when Joe heard Wishbone. He was barking like crazy and jumping around Jimmy's chihuahua.

"Can't you do something about your dog, Talbot?" Damont said, shaking his head in frustration.

"Settle down, Wishbone," Joe called out. *Please,* he added silently. Couldn't Wishbone see this was the most important game of his life?

Wishbone kept barking. Joe frowned as Jimmy's dog, Dinky, trotted over to the sidelines, dragging something in his mouth.

"Just ignore it," Joe said, turning back to Damont. "We're here to play."

"*I'm* here to play," Damont said. "*You're* here to get massacred."

Joe tried to concentrate on the coin toss. But Wishbone's barking was so insistent that Joe had to take another look. "Please be quiet, boy!"

Wishbone was obviously interested in whatever Jimmy's dog had in his mouth. Dinky stopped in front of Jimmy, who was standing on the sidelines. The chihuahua dropped the dirty, shapeless mass to the ground, then scratched Jimmy's sneaker.

Forget about it, Joe told himself. *You've got more important things to do.*

Joe was about to turn back to Damont, when he saw Jimmy glance down and catch sight of the dirty mound. Jimmy's face froze. He dropped quickly to his knees, looking around nervously. Then he grabbed whatever it was and shoved it into his backpack. He acted so . . . suspiciously, Joe couldn't help but take notice.

What was that all about? wondered Joe. Jimmy obviously didn't want anyone to see that thing. But why? What *was* it?

Joe's mind kicked into overdrive. Thinking back, he remembered spotting a dark shape beneath the bushes behind the school, just before he was lured to the tripwire in the woods. What if that *had* been the championship banner, as he'd suspected? And then there was the scrap of blue felt Wishbone had brought into Pepper Pete's. That had definitely come from the banner. Was it possible Jimmy's dog had just brought him the rest of it?

"Earth to Talbot," said Damont. "Can we get this game going?"

Joe was so lost in thought he didn't even look at Damont, much less answer. Joe had assumed whoever had pulled the pranks was the same person who'd stolen the banner. Now he wondered, could it have been *Jimmy* all along, and *not* Damont?

Jimmy *had* acted nervous when Joe had asked him and the other kids about the missing water bottles and equipment. And he'd been uneasy when Joe mentioned the pranks again at Pepper Pete's. Then there was the way Dinky had dropped that thing at Jimmy's feet just now. . . .

Wishbone had done the same thing to Joe countless times when he fetched something. It was almost as if the dog *knew* it was Jimmy's. After all, if it *was* the championship banner, Joe wouldn't expect Dinky to know it didn't belong to Jimmy in the first place.

Hmm, thought Joe. He remembered something else, too. Hadn't he overheard Jimmy tell Damont it was a big mistake that Damont's sneakers had itching powder in them? Joe had assumed Jimmy was just talking big to impress his cousin. But maybe what Jimmy was really trying to say was that he had made a mistake when *he* put the powder in Damont's sneakers. . . .

"We don't have all night." Damont's voice broke into Joe's thoughts again. "Hey, everyone. Looks like Talbot is too chicken to play me."

Joe didn't bother to answer. Crossing his arms over his chest, he strode over to Jimmy. "Mind showing everyone what's in your pack, Jimmy?" he asked.

Wishbone kept up his barking. He was jumping excitedly around Jimmy's pack. Joe almost had the feeling Wishbone *knew* what was in there—and that it was important to Joe.

Jimmy tried unsuccessfully to shoo Wishbone away. The nervous gleam in his eyes made Joe even more suspicious. "Uh . . . well . . . Why should I show *you* anything?" he asked.

"What's going on?" Damont asked, frowning. "*You're* the one with something to hide, Talbot, not Jimmy."

Joe looked down to see Wishbone clamp his teeth around the zipper pull of Jimmy's backpack. As the dog yanked the zipper open, a dirty, dark blue corner of felt popped through the opening. *Hmm . . .* thought Joe. *It's the same color as the Bulldogs's banner. . . .* He decided to take a chance.

"I think Jimmy *does* have something to hide," Joe said. He bent down and tugged the dirty felt through the opening. As he held it up, the triangular shape of the banner was visible. One corner had torn off, along

with part of a gold letter. But the words LEAGUE CHAMPS were still there.

Yes! he thought. *Way to go, Wishbone!* Looking around, he asked aloud, "Does everyone recognize this?"

"It's the championship banner!" Sam exclaimed.

Wishbone's tail was wagging, and he barked up at Joe, as if to say, "Nice detective work, Joe!"

Damont frowned at the banner, then at his cousin. "How did *you* get it, Jimmy?"

Jimmy's mouth fell open. "I . . . uh . . . Dinky dragged it here. I don't know where it came from!"

"That banner has been missing since the pranks began," Joe said. "We all figured whoever pulled those tricks probably took it. Was it you, Jimmy?"

One look at the scared, guilty expression on Jimmy's face, and Joe knew he was right.

"It looks like we've found the prankster, everyone," he said.

Chapter Sixteen

Wishbone barked up happily at Joe. "Good work, buddy! I *told* you that you were as good a detective as Sam Spade. 'Atta boy!"

Wishbone could smell the lies and deceit in Jimmy. The guilty look on the boy's face was a dead giveaway, too. Sitting back on his hind legs, Wishbone waited to hear what Jimmy would say.

"I . . . uh . . ." Jimmy looked around frantically, like a cat who'd been caught up a tree. Finally, he threw up his hands and said, "Okay! Okay! I did it."

"See? I *told* you guys Joe was innocent!" Wishbone circled past Joe's teammates, wagging his tail. Then he stopped next to Joe. Sam and David came over, too, and they were both smiling. But when Wishbone turned to Damont, there was a scowl on the boy's face.

"*You* pulled those tricks? The itching powder? And the soap?" Damont asked. When Jimmy nodded, Damont gave an annoyed shake of his head. "But why? I could have broken a leg!"

Damont didn't seem concerned about the other

players, Wishbone noticed. "Oh, well. Nothing new there. But Jimmy, *why* did you do it?"

Jimmy looked at Damont, and his face turned bright red. "I did it for you, Damont!" he exclaimed.

Wishbone blinked in surprise. "Come again?"

"Wait a second. Back up," said Joe. "You put itching powder in Damont's sneakers. And you rubbed soap where he stepped in it. How is that supposed to *help* him?"

"That was a mistake," said Jimmy, grimacing.

"You lost me," said David. "Maybe you should start at the beginning, Jimmy."

Jimmy took a deep breath. "Well, Damont is the best basketball player in the whole school," he began. "That's why my friends and I come to the gym to watch practices after school—to see him in action." His face was bright red and he kept his eyes focused on the ground as he spoke. "It really bugged me when people started making a big deal about some of the other players."

"Like Joe?" Sam asked.

Jimmy shot a cloudy glance at Joe and nodded. "Damont is a better player than you," he said.

"Joe's been playing really well," Drew spoke up, frowning. "We all have. Maybe Damont sinks more shots than the rest of us, but he can't win on his own."

"Hear, hear!" Wishbone wagged his tail and barked up at the guys on the team. "You need one another—*and* your official mascot."

"Drew's right," added Hank. "The Bulldogs are having a great season because we're *all* playing well.

We *were,* anyway . . . until you started in with those pranks, Jimmy."

"Yeah. What's your problem?" Damont asked.

Jimmy's eyes flashed with embarrassment. "I . . . I thought if I did things to make the other guys look bad, people would remember *you're* the star of the team, Damont," said Jimmy. "Everything went okay when I hid the water bottles and knee pads and stuff. But the day after that, when I put itching powder in everyone's sneakers, I guess I got mixed up. I put the powder in your sneakers instead of—"

"In mine," Joe finished.

Wishbone gazed back and forth between Joe's sneakers and Damont's. Both pairs were blue-and-white, brand-new, and super-high-tech. Even a dog might have made the same mistake. Well, that solved one mystery. . . .

"After that, I tried to be more careful," Jimmy went on. "I rubbed the soap on the floor, next to the bleachers where Joe always puts his towel—"

"But I was late that day, so I didn't put my stuff there," Joe put in. He shook his head in amazement. "I was practically the only who *didn't* step in that soap."

"What about the tin of itching powder Wishbone found behind the school?" Drew asked Jimmy. "Did you put it there?"

Wishbone cocked his head to one side, looking up at Jimmy. "You must have set up that string in the woods, too! *And* lured Joe and me back there. That was *not* nice, Jimmy."

"I dumped the tin out back to get rid of it," Jimmy explained. "When I saw Joe looking around later, I figured he was trying to find out who did it. I didn't want him to find out it was me, so . . ." He hesitated, shooting a glance at Marcus. "Well, I took Marcus's cap, and—"

"What!" Marcus exclaimed.

"You dropped it while we were watching practice," Jimmy said. "Anyway, I set up a string to trip Joe, to give me time to escape. Then I put the hat on and made sure Joe saw it. When he chased me back there, I put the hat in the bushes near the string, and then ran away."

"But . . . why?" Marcus interrupted.

Sam frowned at Jimmy and said, "Because he wanted Joe to think *you* lured him into the woods, and that you were the prankster."

"That was a serious prank, Jimmy. I could have been hurt," Joe pointed out. "Would you have let Marcus take the blame even then?"

Jimmy shrugged and looked down at the ground. "I didn't think you would get hurt. I just wanted to make sure I had time to get away."

"I thought you were my friend, Jimmy." Marcus looked insulted and confused, and Wishbone understood why. He knew firsthand how terrible it felt to be betrayed, thanks to his experience with Yorkie.

"How did you snatch the championship banner?" Joe asked.

"I saw it hanging on the wall when I went to hide the knee pads and water bottles," Jimmy explained. "I guess I got carried away with the idea of taking stuff. On the spur of the moment, I grabbed the banner, too." He looked around sheepishly before continuing.

"I meant to give it back. But after I got home, Dinky got hold of it. I didn't see it again—until now."

"And the rest . . ."—Wishbone picked up one corner of the banner in his mouth and shook it—". . . is history!"

"Do you know how much trouble you caused me?" Damont said. "The Bulldogs could lose tomorrow because of what you've done!"

Wishbone noticed Damont didn't take any responsibility for his own actions. Apparently, Damont didn't think turning the entire team against Joe had anything to do with the problems the team had been having on the court.

"Sorry," Jimmy mumbled.

"That's not good enough," Sam said, stepping forward. "I think you owe a public apology to Joe, the coach—"

"Does *he* have to know about this?" Damont spoke up quickly. "I mean, why get Coach Allen involved? Jimmy already said he was sorry."

"The coach has a right to know what really happened," Hank pointed out. "Besides, it's not fair to Joe to keep it quiet. People should know he wasn't responsible for any of this stuff that happened."

Damont scowled but said nothing. He obviously didn't care about restoring Joe's reputation. After all, now everyone would know that Damont's cousin was the guilty one *and* that Damont had blamed Joe unfairly all along.

"Maybe next time you'll think twice before accusing my pal Joe of foul play." Wishbone trotted over to Joe and sat down next to him, his tail wagging. "Now, why don't we put all of this behind us and concentrate on tomorrow's game?"

"Let's hear it for the Bulldogs!" Wishbone trotted along the sidelines in his mascot's sweater the next afternoon. The Bulldogs and the Bobcats had two minutes left to play in the first half. With two quarters still left to play, it was one of the most exciting games Wishbone had ever seen.

The crowd cheered as Drew dribbled the ball down the court for the Bulldogs. Glancing into the stands, Wishbone saw Ellen and Sam among the students and families packed into the bleachers.

As Drew hurled the ball through the air, Ellen rose to her feet and shouted, "Come on, Joe!"

A second later, Joe's hands closed firmly around the ball. Wishbone stayed tensely alert as the Bobcats closed in. "You can outsmart those felines, Joe! No problem!"

Joe faked left, then passed right to Damont. The crowd roared as Damont grabbed the ball, then jumped for the shot from mid-court.

"That's good for three points, by Damont Jones," David said into the microphone at the announcer's table, and his amplified voice echoed through the gym. "Bobcats, thirty-five; Bulldogs, thirty-one."

"Thanks to a great assist by Joe Talbot! Way to go Joe!" Wishbone barked his best cheer and wagged his tail proudly. "Looks like you boys nailed that combination after all."

Wishbone jumped out of the way as Coach Allen strode to the sidelines.

"Good offense! Keep it up, team." The coach formed a T with his hands. Wishbone knew this meant he wanted the players to call a time-out. Seconds later, Damont made the request and the referee blew his whistle.

As the players huddled on the sidelines, Wishbone wove between their feet. "Good team effort, guys! But being a mascot sure can make a dog thirsty." He glanced up as Jimmy hustled from the bleachers with water bottles for the players. "How about one of those for man's best friend?"

Wishbone had been on hand before the game when Jimmy had apologized to Coach Allen and the team for pulling the pranks. Coach Allen had decided

not to report Jimmy to school officials. In return, Jimmy had agreed to be the team's water boy for the next month.

"Here you go, Damont," Jimmy said. He handed over a water bottle, an eager smile on his face. Damont snatched it away, without even glancing at Jimmy.

"You could at least say 'thank you,' Damont." Wishbone hurried to lap up the spray that spilled from the players' bottles. "Maybe if you paid more attention to Jimmy, he wouldn't have to try so hard to impress you in the first place."

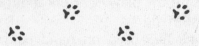

Joe had just made a two-point layup shot when the buzzer sounded to end the first half of the game. The Bulldogs were still down by one point, but Joe had a good feeling. The team was playing well together. Joe thought they might be able to pull off a win, after all.

As he and the other boys jogged toward the locker room, the home-team crowd jumped to their feet, cheering and clapping.

"Take five to cool off," said Coach Allen. "Then I want to talk strategy for the second half."

The coach started for the door, but as he passed Joe, he paused to say, "That was some nice teamwork out there, boys. I'm proud of the way you put your troubles behind you and came together. Keep up the good work." The coach spoke to all of them, but as he said the word *teamwork,* he'd looked right at Joe.

Joe felt as if he would burst with pride. As Joe opened his locker, Wishbone trotted over in his blue-and-gold Sequoyah Bulldogs sweater. The terrier looked up at Joe with bright eyes, his tail wagging, as if to say, "I'm proud of you, too!"

As Joe grabbed his towel, he spotted his dad's copy of *The Maltese Falcon* at the bottom of his locker. Lying and double-crossing hadn't worked for the people in Dashiell Hammett's mystery. Brigid O'Shaughnessy had killed Sam Spade's partner in order to keep the Maltese falcon, and she'd wound up in jail. The other characters had been just as unscrupulous, and they, too, had wound up in jail—or even dead.

Sam Spade was the only character in the whole book who had stuck to the principles he felt were right. And in the end, the police and everyone else came to realize Spade hadn't committed the crimes they'd suspected of him.

"Just like me," Joe said, ruffling Wishbone's fur behind his ears. "Sam Spade got to the bottom of his mystery by paying attention to details and trusting his instincts about people. In the end, I guess that's how you and I found the prankster here at Sequoyah, too. Thanks, Wishbone."

With a bark, Wishbone picked up *The Maltese Falcon* in his mouth and shook it playfully. It was as if he were trying to tell Joe something about the story.

It sure feels good to have a friend I know I can count on, no matter what, thought Joe. "You heard the coach. Let's take five, Wishbone." Joe grinned, scratching the terrier behind his ears. "We've earned it."

About Anne Capeci

Anne Capeci is a freelance writer who has published more than a dozen books for children and young adults. She loves to read and write mysteries, but *The Maltese Dog* is the first one she's written that features a canine detective. Creating a mystery for Wishbone was such a fun challenge that Anne is already hard at work on a second WISHBONE mystery, *Key to the Golden Dog*.

Like Wishbone and Joe, Anne was fascinated by the story of *The Maltese Falcon*. Dashiell Hammett wrote about a world filled with greed, suspicion, and betrayal. In searching out the truth about the Maltese falcon, Detective Sam Spade had many opportunities to be greedy and dishonest himself. Yet he never hesitated to do the right thing—even when that meant other people thought he was guilty of wrongdoing. In writing *The Maltese Dog*, Anne wanted to explore how kids—and dogs—would handle a similar situation.

Anne lives in Brooklyn, New York, with her husband, Jonathan Fabricant, and their two children, Daniel and Marissa. They would like someday to have a dog of their own—if their mischievous cat, Cleo, will let them. Their house is more than a hundred years old, with creaky stairways, uneven floors, a dusty cellar, and a backyard where they have found old glass bottles and an Indian arrowhead. Living there gives Anne plenty of material for many mysteries to come.

Appear in a WISHBONE™ Mystery!

One lucky winner (age seven through twelve) will have the chance to help Wishbone™ solve a mystery by appearing in an upcoming WISHBONE Mysteries book! The winner will have his or her photograph on the front cover of a future book, a role in the story, and his or her likeness in an illustration in the text. Enter today! Simply hand-print your name, address, birthday, and your favorite mystery story of all time on a 3"-by-5" card, or on the official entry blank available at participating retailers. Mail to:

WISHBONE • BIG FEATS! ENTERTAINMENT • ATTN: MYSTERY SERIES SWEEPSTAKES
P.O. BOX 3472 • YOUNG AMERICA, MN 55558-3472

Coming Soon!

The SUPER Adventures of
WISHBONE

#1

Dog Days
OF THE
WEST

By Vivian Sathre
Inspired by *Heart of the West* by O. Henry

WHAT HAS FOUR LEGS, A HEALTHY COAT, AND A GREAT DEAL ON MEMBERSHIP?

IT'S THE WISHBONE ZONE™
THE OFFICIAL WISHBONE™ FAN CLUB!

When you enter the **WISHBONE ZONE,** you get:
- Color poster of **Wishbone**™
- **Wishbone** newsletter filled with photos, news, and games
- Autographed photo of **Wishbone** and his friends
- **Wishbone** sunglasses, and more!

To join the fan club, pay $10 and charge your **WISHBONE ZONE** membership to VISA, MasterCard, or Discover. Call:

1-800-888-WISH

Or send us your name, address, phone number, birth date, and a check for $10 payable to Big Feats! (TX residents add $.83 sales tax/IN residents add $.50 sales tax). Write to:

WISHBONE ZONE
P.O. Box 9523
Allen, TX 75013-9523

Prices and offer are subject to change. Place your order now!

Now Playing on Your VCR...

Two exciting **Wishbone®** stories on video!

Ready for an adventure? Then leap right in with **Wishbone™** as he takes you on a thrilling journey through two great action-packed stories. First, there are haunted houses, buried treasure, and mysterious graves in two back-to-back episodes of *A Tail in Twain*, starring **Wishbone** as Tom Sawyer. Then, no one is more powerful than **Wishbone**, in *Hercules Unleashed*, featuring exciting new footage! It's more fun than a flea dip! It's **Wishbone** on home video.

Available wherever videos are sold.